ISBN: 9798479767180

Cover design by: Art Painter
Library of Congress Control
Number: 2018675309

For my parents Jim and Jean, who took us all on a grand adventure. For my kids: Neal, Stef, Annah, Jenna, and Annie. For my husband, the tech genius. For my sister Carolyn who is my best friend and biggest supporter. And last but not least… to my Daddy in heaven… I finally did it! Love, your Jannie

Introduction

∞∞∞

Kate Asher has a painful secret from her past. Already a widow at age 42, she presses on to start a new life. Ten years after her husband was killed in a plane crash. Escaping to a cabin home on a lake in Northern Minnesota, Kate discovers the delights of small town living and the personalities that come with it. Eventually her secret catches up to her and her world crashes. But sometimes good things come to those who wait. Pour yourself a cup of tea, grab a scone and curl up with this sweet story of love and reconciliation

New Beginnings
on
Cedarcrest Lake

An old gentleman observed quite a ruckus going on that night at the River's Edge supper club at the corner table. A woman and two men spoke with great animation and emotion. Tears rolling down their faces but smiling. He wondered what all the fuss was about.

∞∞∞∞∞∞∞∞∞∞

CHAPTER 1

It was nearly the 10th anniversary of her husband's death in a small plane crash that killed Ken and his three buddies on the way to a fishing trip in Canada. Kate Asher had become a widow along with her three friends at the age of 42. Two of the women had re-married but she and Rose had gone on alone. With two kids to raise on her own and left with a broken heart she was finally ready, now that the kids were both grown and on their own paths, to restart her life. She was done being in the 'Widow's Club'.

Kate looked over her new 'cabin' on Cedarcrest Lake in Northern Minnesota and sighed. At last, she was here! The insurance money after her husband died plus the money she had earned as an author, was helping her achieve her lifelong goal. Living in the country near a small town and being able to finally have time to herself to write. After all she had been through in the last ten years, she felt ready to let go and to try to move on without Ken.

Not really a cabin, but a house and a fixer upper with good bones, this place was going to be a labor of love. She was going to be able to do the light stuff like cutting the grass and maintaining the yard but would have to hire out for the inside stuff. Late August and the sun was warm this morning. She had brought the last of her things in late last night and was able to get her bed made up in order to fall into an exhausted sleep. After a trip to the grocery store last night, she was now fully stocked up in the kitchen. Kate loved to cook and was having fun organizing her spice cupboard and setting things up just the way she liked it. She loved to cook, and visions of fresh pasta filled her mind, and she couldn't wait to make her first meal in her new home. For now, the aroma of fresh coffee filled the room and she looked around until she found the box marked KITCHEN GLASSES AND MUGS. Finding the box at last and of course on the bottom of the pile, she ripped off the tape and found the biggest cup. Filling it to an inch below the top so she could add her half and half, she took the cup of coffee and headed out to the screened porch on the back of the house that faced the lake. As she pushed on the door it detached from the rusty hinges and fell flat into the porch with a loud bang. "Well, there is chore number one!" she thought sighing. She sat on her new wicker couch with the pretty, fluffy, cushions and sighed as she gazed out at her new 'yard.' Peace filled her heart and she thanked God for her new place, her new beginning, and saying goodbye to a past she no longer had to endure. The water shimmered like diamonds as the morning sun shone on the calm lake this morning and a pair of loons beckoned to each other from the south side of the lake. Big, white cumulus clouds dotted the sky. Kate took in all the sights and smells of her new lake home. The air was fresh and clean.

Her dear friend Angie, a successful real estate agent up here in the north, had been put on notice two years ago, that she was looking for a year-round lake home. Out of the blue she had called Kate three months ago saying that an older couple and dear friends of hers from church were looking to sell and move south to get away from the harsh Minnesota winters. A kindly retired couple were looking for just the 'right' person for their cabin and Angie had told them about Kate and her story and they had met for coffee several times before they decided to deed the house to her without it ever going on the market and she got the house for a great price. Angie had worked another miracle. She saw this yet as another sign from God that she was doing the right thing and was on the right path. The cabin was in good shape but needed some updating. With money set aside for such tasks, it was just a matter of finding the right person for the job. Looking down at her now empty cup she felt ready to tackle the big job of unpacking. She grabbed a blueberry muffin, scarfed it down and got to work.

Hours later, her kitchen was all put together complete with fresh flowers from the yard on her old wooden farm table. Kate was a collector of old furniture. Not fancy antiques but old farm furniture. She loved the dents in the table that told stories of lives past, imagining families around the table making memories. Most of her furniture was like this and she had taken great care and time over the years for just the right pieces. She had even found a headboard for her bed at an estate sale made from barn wood that was over one hundred years old. She loved the charm when old and new were brought together. History past and present. Kate loved the open floor plan. One big room with the living room and dining room and kitchen, a full bathroom and laundry room and a screened porch off the back of the dining room, with French doors leading out, off the screened porch was a large deck with three steps down to the yard that led to the lake. There were three bedrooms in total and another full bathroom upstairs. The master bedroom being upstairs in the large loft like area. She loved the idea of waking up to the lake view every morning with the full wall of windows that went to the ceiling. She began to haul boxes of the clothes and toiletries up and by the late afternoons she was too tired to move. Tummy growling, she grabbed some cold cuts, cheese and red grapes from the fridge and opened a bottle of Pine Gorgio. Throwing everything together on a tray she went back out to the screened in porch stepping carefully over the door. First thing tomorrow she would head to the hardware store to get some new hinges and some other necessary things and familiarize herself with her new little town four miles from her new home.

After sleeping better than she had in years, Kate woke up to the sounds of lake life, boat motors buzzing as early morning fishing was getting under way and the loons sang their morning songs. The sun streamed through her tall windows and kissed her face with its warmth. Kate stretched and threw off her light quilt and headed to the bathroom for a quick shower and a touch of make –up, throwing her medium length chestnut hair up in a quick messy doo. Going to her large closet she chose a turquoise sun dress and some strappy silver sandals. After a quick look in the mirror, she headed down the to the kitchen for a cup of coffee and a light breakfast of fruit and some toast. List in hand, she headed out to her car not bothering to lock up. She was in the country now and was told by locals that no one broke into your house up here. There was a slight haze in the air today as the temps started to heat up and she was glad she was getting to town early before the heat set in.

Like a picture taken out of the old west, this little town was charming to say the least. Large flower planters lined both side of the five-block main street and American flags proudly flew on each corner. Little shops lined the streets with a bakery, Sue's Café, a boutique, a small salon, a hardware store, an old school five and dime, Grants Groceries next to the Café and Gas stations on each end of town. Throw in some antique stores, plus a small office building with various businesses completed the little town on main street. Big box stores were twenty miles away if you needed big stuff, but Kate really wanted to be part of this community and was happy to support local businesses. There were also two bars, one on either side of the road and one, called Lu Lu's had a sign saying, 'Karaoke every Friday Night!' Kate thought this sounded fun but for now her focus was on the hardware store and finding someone who could help her get that door fixed.

Opening the door, the bell at the top gave a ring alerting the owners that someone had entered the store. The old building had dark wood floors that squeaked with her every step. 'They don't need a bell to let someone know that you're here!' Kate laughed to herself. As if on cue a man called out, "Hey, can I help you with something?" Kate turned at the sound of the voice and there stood a man about 6 feet tall, salt and pepper hair and kind eyes. Huh, this guy is handsome she thought, kind of a Kevin Costner type if you squinted your eyes.

"Hey, are you ok?" said the guy noticing her squinting. Kate blushed from head to toe and snapped out of her assessment of the man.

" Uh, Oh yes, sorry!! Um I just moved close to here a few days ago and I need to pick up a few things." She glanced at his name tag, and it said "Grant" Grant laughed and said, "are you the one who bought the Peterson place out on Cedarcrest Lake?" Knowing how small towns are, replied that yes, she was the 'one'. Grant looked to be around her age and smiled and said "Welcome! Now what do you need help with?"

In the last ten years Kate's focus had been on being there for her grieving kids and just getting through the long days. When a spouse that you loved has died, you live in the place of what if. What if Ken were here for 'this?' How would Ken have wanted her to handle 'that'? It had taken so long to stop thinking that the accident was a mistake and Ken would be back someday to carry on with their lives. She had cried herself to sleep for the first year and had to force herself to keep getting up every day so that she could be there for the kids. The oldest Harry, now 28 was living out his dream as a Master Gardener and had his own thriving landscaping business down in the Twin Cities and Addie, at 26 lived with her best friend and was a special education teacher. Proud of both of her kids, Kate finally took their advice to start living her own life. So right in front of her was Mr. Handsome. Her thoughts went off in all sorts of directions when thinking of things, he could 'help' with. Laughing to herself she finally blurted out that she needed some screws. REALLY??? That's what came out of her mouth? Hinges!!! She needed hinges! Oh my god, she thought, what is wrong with me? Grant raised his eyebrows at her and laughed. After telling him about her situation with the door and a few other odds and ends she needed supplies for, she paid for her purchases at the checkout counter and grabbed her bags to leave. As she reached for the old brass doorknob, Grant called after her "Hey if you need a handy man, I do jobs on the side when things are slow around here." Not believing her luck, he walked over with a card with his contact info on it. It looked legit. It was corny though. It said, "Let me GRANT your wishes". UM OK…. yeah, maybe NOT. Definitely not her type. Faking a HUGE smile, Kate thanked the man and quickly ran to her car to dump off her goods and look around the town.

The smell of fresh baked bread wafting through the breeze stopped Kate in her tracks and she turned an about face and headed in the direction of the bakery. Another bell at the top of the door let the locals know a new face was in town as many faces turned to see who was coming in the door. Not one to shy away, Kate made her way to the counter as the locals checked her out from head to toe. She turned around and took a deep breath and smiled at everyone. To her surprise people were genuinely happy and smiled back at her and greeted her warmly. She introduced herself to Ashley, the gal at the counter and owner of the bakery. From what Kate could tell looked to be in her mid-40's. Ashley looked like she was a hippy right out of the 70's. From her long kinky, strawberry blond hair, the crystal earrings she wore in her ears, bejeweled rings on every finger, a gauzy long flowing off white top and old faded jeans with holes here and there worn by time. Her shop was filled with crystals that hung from the windows and on each little table were bowls of beautiful colored rocks. Hand painted barn wood signs hung on the walls with sayings like LIFE IS GOOD, and LOVE LOVE LOVE and EAT YOUR FEELINGS. She had a bit of flour on her pierced nose to top off the scene. Ashley made her way to the counter. "Hey Kate, we were all just talking about you seeing that you went into the hardware store." See what I mean, Kate thought? But this is what she wanted. The small-town thing. Ashley laughed and said "sorry, we were hoping we would be able to meet you knowing that eventually you'd get hungry and have to come to town and we were all excited to meet you after Angie told us you bought the Peterson place! There were dear friends of this community, and we were all curious to see who they thought was the special person they chose to move into their place." Kate felt somewhat pressured at having to be the 'someone special'.

"Well thanks everyone for the welcome, I'm so happy to meet all of you and am looking forward to being a part of your community! She said smiling and hoped no one noticed the sweat breaking out on her forehead. She didn't much care for being the center of attention. After meeting a few more people, the bakery emptied out and Kate was finally able to feast her eyes on the pastry case. Like a rich woman in a jewelry store looking over diamonds, Kate saw the most beautiful baked goods she had ever seen! She did a quick look around.... oh ....my .... god .... was she in France? Her mouth watered as she gazed at row after row of stunning pastries. There was not a doughnut in sight! One of her favorite pastries in the world was a Danish with almond paste, covered in roasted slivered almonds and it lay before her like a long-lost lover beckoning to her from behind the counter. Her eyes traveled down the case, and she saw chocolate filled croissants, layer after buttery perfect layer of the thin pastry, dark chocolate oozing out of the middle, mini tarts with fresh raspberries, blueberries and chocolate shined with a high gloss sheen. Canelés, the soft little pastry perfumed with vanilla and hint of rum called to her like a whisper in the wind. Macaroons the colors of the rainbow proudly lay in prefect rows and towards the end of the pastry case were perfect loaves of Brioche, a soft and sweet bread that went perfect with strawberry jam and a good cup of tea. "I have died and gone to heaven" sigh Kate. Baking had been one of her passions, but she had never come close to doing anything such as these beautiful pieces of edible art. After what felt like hours of food lusting, Ashley, watching her with a big smile on her face finally said "Well? How was it?" Kate looked up slightly embarrassed at being busted in her food lust. But Ashely said "Hey! Don't be embarrassed! That is why I do this!

Life is short and you need to do what you love, and I love to watch the pleasure on people's faces when people eat my pastries. So, what is your pleasure Madame? The first one in on me because I know once you have one you will be a customer for life.

"Please oh Please let me start with the almond Danish" Kate said with the enthusiasm of a child at the fair. Wait, was that drool coming out of her mouth? She quickly wiped it away before anyone saw it.

"If know what I think I know about you, you're going to want this with a good old cup of strong British tea, cream and sugar right?" Ashley said. Kate knew at this moment that she had a new friend for life. She got her Danish and tea and sat at a tiny corner table in the shop front and took her first bite of the almond Danish, she closed her eyes and savored it on her tongue. Making yummy noise like hmm, oh lord yes, and long sighs! She was sounding like the fake orgasm noises Meg Ryan had made in 'When Harry Met Sally', and she failed to notice the light tapping on her shoulder…

"Err excuse me. Uh sorry to interrupt" the deep sexy male voice said, finally reaching her Danish induced deaf ears. Shaking herself out of the trance, she opened her eyes and looked up, wait, more up, to a very good-looking man with salt and pepper hair, deep blue eyes and looking very fit. Something looked familiar about him. Huh. Minding her drool, she waited ……she was unable to speak. Her mouth hung open like a baby bird waiting for its first meal. Phew! This guy did something to her insides.

"Uh sorry to interrupt your um personal time, (he snickered !!!) but I left my jacket here and you are sitting on it" Said TDH (tall dark and handsome). What is it with this town? The two men she meets right off the bat are out of the ordinary handsome! Must be something in the water, Kate thought while staring at this perhaps Danish induced mirage. Feeling a hot flash coming on Kate quickly stood up knocking over her chair complete with TDH's jacket breaking its fall on the floor.

"oh my gosh I am so sorry!!! I was just enjoying my Danish! I can just imagine what *that* sounded like!" Kate said with a nervous laugh. Nervous laugh? What the hell!! She was 52 years old and not a high school kid! As she bent over to pick up the chair and jacket he had also leaned down at the same time and both went to grab the jacket at the same time. As if hit by a tiny bolt of lightning as their hands touched, she quickly pulled back, whoa, what was that??? He seemed a little stunned himself.

"Hi, I'm Drew and you?"

"Hey, I'm Kate and sorry about your jacket". They shook hands, both seeming to feel that little jolt again. "Well, nice to meet you!" he said and then before he left, he looked back at her another time hesitating and then the tiny bell rang as he left the bakery. Sighing, she sat back down and watched as he walked down the street to his car. Lord that man was good looking and he kind of reminded her of someone. Snapping back to reality, she sipped her yummy tea and finished her Danish, grabbed her bag of Brioche, she headed back out to her place.

On the drive home she couldn't get Drew out of her head. He seemed familiar to her. But that was impossible. Maybe someone from down in the cities? Having been alone for the last ten years she wondered what it would be like to be in a relationship again and she knew Ken would want her to find someone to grow old with. She teared up once again knowing it wasn't going to be him. But NO, she was NOT going back to that way of thinking! Staying in the past and the 'what if's' was not healthy. She had a new future and a lot to look forward to on this new adventure. Pulling in her driveway she found an older woman in white jean shorts and a very loud flowery shirt peering in her side door window that led into the kitchen. Getting out of her car and shutting the door a little more loudly than necessary, the woman startled and turned around towards Kate.

"Oh, hello there! I'm Jan, you're neighbor! I was just stopping by to bring you some dinner and welcome you to Cedarcrest Lake!" Jan ran down the three steps towards Kate and surprised her by bringing her in for a hug. Jan was a very nice-looking woman. With a head of beautiful gray hair and a trim figure, kind blue eyes and an infectious smile. Kate guessed her to be in her early 70's.

"Oh well OK!!! Nice to meet you, Jan!" Kate said with a laugh. Jan told she had lived here for 20 years and that her friend Jean who had sold her the house had been best buddies for all the time they had lived here. She was going to miss her friend dearly. Kate led the way into the house and set her purchases on the counter with Jan following behind her.

"I figured you would be too exhausted after your move to fix anything to eat so I made you a tuna casserole. I'll stick it in the fridge for you and you can just heat it up anytime you get hungry. I would love to help you unpack if you need me, my family is all gone and It's just me now, I lost my husband Frank a year ago to cancer so I'm always looking for something to do." She said with a smile that held some grief. Kate smiled and was pleased to have a woman nearby to talk to and understood the loneliness that can come from being a widow...

"Well, first of all thanks so much for the meal! You are right I have a lot of work to do on this main floor today and I would love some help if you were serious about your offer. How about we start with the living room? The movers did all the furniture, but I have all the other stuff to unpack. I finished unpacking my room and the bathroom upstairs." Jan rushed over for another hug and asked where to start. Kate led the way to the pile of boxes stacked up in the corner of the living room and they spent the rest of the afternoon unpacking the rest of her things. They even got some pictures put up on the walls. Kate looked around and seeing her things laid out just like she liked them, the place was really starting to feel like her home. By 6 pm they were both tired and had spent the afternoon listening to great music from the 60's and 70's, singing along and laughing at some of the oldie moldies. Kate felt so comfortable with this easy-going gal.

"Say Jan, why don't you stay for dinner? You must be tired too and I'd love the company. I'll open a bottle of wine and we can sit out on the porch and watch the sun go down. By the way does a Shiraz go ok with tuna casserole? Kate said laughing out loud. Jan stared at her, and her eyes filled with tears.

"I would love to stay and yes Shiraz goes perfectly with tuna casserole and probably anything else you make" she said warmly. Kate threw together a salad and sliced some fresh bread.

Rubbing their stomachs in satisfaction, and the bottle of wine almost gone the two women gazed contentedly out at the lake. They had shared a lot about each other during the meal and Kate felt like she had not only a new friend but a mother figure. Having been on the outs with her mom for years, she loved the idea of having this sweet older woman in her life. Jan similarly had always longed for a daughter. She and Frank had been unable to have children and Jan and Frank had become grandparents to many of the kids that came up to the cabins on the weekends. By 9 pm both ladies were tired and ready for bed. Kate thanked Jan for all of her help and for the dinner and the new friendship as she hugged the nice-looking woman and said goodnight. On the way-out Jan said "Oh, by the way, the people that live here year-round take a boat ride every night around 7pm. We call it a 'putt putt'. We all line up and go around the lake and watch the sun go down. I go with some friends down the way and I'm sure they wouldn't mind having you go along if you're interested."

"That sounds wonderful", Kate explained, "but I have the pontoon that came with the place, and I need to familiarize myself with it, so for now, I will take a rain check. Thanks, and see you tomorrow! Please come for coffee in the morning, I have the most glorious Brioche we can have with some jam." With that Jan bid her goodnight and made the short walk home next door.

After a soak in her big tub adding some lavender Epsom salt and a big squeeze of her favorite bubbles, Kate's sore muscles began to relax. With a sigh of contentment, she dried off in a big fluffy towel, got in her PJ's and fell instantly asleep. It had truly been a full day.

CHAPTER 2

A loud clap of thunder shook Kate awake in the morning thunderstorm passing through the area. She had slept late this morning. Stretching, she planned out her day. Around 9, there was a knock on the kitchen door and a YOOOOOO HOOOO! "Come in Jan!" Yelled Kate from upstairs. Jan shook off her umbrella and set if by the kitchen door and he women sat in the living room and had coffee and some delicious brioche and talked for about an hour. Jan filled her in about the people that lived on the lake year-round and some of the week enders. As Jan left Kate noticed the sun was coming out. It was going to be a beautiful day. Jan hugged her again and off she went with plans of her own for the day. Kate still needed to find someone to fix the porch door and the other little jobs that needed to be done around the house. She fingered that card that she had gotten from Grant. But she just didn't want the guy in her house. She had forgotten to ask Jan if she knew anyone. For now, she wanted to tackle the boat. Kate had had some experience with boats having grown up going to her grandparent's cabin on Lake Osakis. She stopped in the little garage first and picked up the gas cans she had filled in town yesterday. Walking down the small incline to the dock, she added gas to the pontoon. Happy that the dock was in great condition and the boat was only four years old. Again, thanking God for her blessings, she started the boat and backed away for the dock. Taking it slowly to get to know the boat and feel the size of it, she made her way around the lake. It wasn't a huge lake but perfect for what she was looking for. As she rounded a corner the little island in the middle of the lake came into view. Lots of people would park their boats there to swim and someone had put up a long rope on top of hill to swing into the water. She drove past slowing watching a bunch of teens squealing with laughter and flying off the rope into the water. She did NOT see herself doing that, no way. Gliding through the water at a slow pace, Kate lost herself in her thoughts. She really needed to finish her latest book and was struggling to come up with some fresh ideas. Shaken her out of her thoughts, the pontoon started to sputter and gasp and then the engine just stopped…in the middle of the lake…...and she had forgotten her cell phone…. what…. in… the……… she tried to start the motor to no avail and looking around she saw the Island in the distance, but that was too far away, no one would hear her. A speed boat passed by pulling a water skier and she waved her hands frantically, but they just thought she was waving at them and waved back yelling "HI!" Okay that wasn't going to work. With her hand flat over her eyebrows, she scanned the lake looking for someone who might be able to help her.

"Hello? Do you need some help?" A sexy voice said flowing over the waves. Kate looked behind her and TDH had quietly pulled his fishing boat up next to the back of her pontoon. Oh my god, WHY did HE have to be the one! It seemed as if he always caught her in embarrassing moments. Sighing, Kate stepped to the back of the pontoon and nervously said "um yes I think I do! I was just taking my boat out for the first time and the engine just quit and I forgot my phone back at my place".

"Hey I remember you!" said TDH. "From the bakery, right? Let me come on board and see if I can find the trouble if that's ok with you?"

"Sure, that would be great, if it's no trouble." Kate said blushing to her toes. She wanted to take all this bloody blushing and throw it in the lake! Her hormones betrayed her feelings on a regular basis.

"No trouble at all." When he smiled the sun seemed to dim. He was so handsome!! She ran a hand through her hair and wondered if she had even brushed it that day, she hadn't bothered with any make up either. Not to self: Always do something with your hair and put on a little make up in case you run in to handsome stranger. Kate rolled her eyes about her self-talk. He dropped anchor on his boat and climbed on the swimming deck off the back her pontoon and grabbed the railing as a boat sped by causing TDH to lose his balance and fall into Kate, accidently grabbing one of her ample breasts as he went down.

"Oh my gosh are you okay?" Kate asked yet another dreaded hot flash turn her face and neck bright red. Those steel blues eyes looked up at her as he helped himself up and said "Am I okay? I just used your breast as a handle!! I am so sorry for how that fall went, not the best impression, sorry!" He palmed his head and shook it back and forth. "Geez!!"

"Well, I can be a handful!" Kate said, wonderful, just wonderful! Why did she say THAT? Adding to the already weird conversation. "I'm just glad you're okay. Now, let's figure out what is going on with this boat!" Kate said with a big smile, wanting to move on from the boob topic. After a few minutes of inspecting things, he told her that the boat had no oil in it. Well, GEEZ, you have to have oil!!! She felt embarrassed that she had not checked on that. Maybe she wasn't as equipped to handle this boat as she thought. She might need a few lessons.... maybe from him? YUM!

"I just moved here, and the boat came with the place, and I was just taking it out for a quick spin before the locals go out for their boat parade tonight. I never thought to check the oil. I really appreciate you helping me. I'm pretty embarrassed about it and I'm so glad you stopped to help." Kate said dropping her anchor.

TDH nodded sympathetically and said "well, you're not quite done with me yet, I'm going to have to tow you back to your place because I don't have any boat oil on me".

"Let me check and see if there is any on board." Kate checked and there was no oil.

"Oh geez, no oil in the bin either. I am so sorry! Thanks for the help, I really appreciate it!" She was quickly becoming the 'damsel in distress'. She didn't want that role ……. unless it came attached to this handsome guy!

"Well, I can't leave a damsel in distress, or my Mom would have my hide!" Wait, had he just read her thoughts? After about twenty minutes, TDH had her boat tied to his he began to tow her back to her dock. It took about a half an hour as it was the middle of the afternoon and lots of people were out enjoying their boats and pulling tubers, skiers, and fishing. Having safely gotten her boat back to the dock. TDH tied his boat off and climbed up on her dock.

"I cannot thank you enough for all the help you've me this afternoon and I'm sorry if I ruined your fishing" Kate said thankfully.

"Actually, I have a cooler full of sonnies and a few walleyes, so I was on my way home. And I still need to put some oil in that boat, so you are good to go for the parade tonight." Drew said with a kind smile.

Kate needed to start using his real name in her head. TDH seemed disrespectful for this kind man. He had been so helpful today. And he had touched her boob! She chuckled to herself. No longer feeling like a stranger, Drew reached over the pontoon and held out a strong hand to help her off the boat. Once again, she felt a shock and shiver from the top of her head all the ways to her toes. "Drew, you have been so kind to help me out this afternoon, how about I clean those fish and make you some dinner as a thank you?" Kate's pretty Hershey kisses brown eyes lit up as she smiled up at his handsome face. Clean fish? She thought to herself, she hadn't cleaned a fish in 30 years!

"Oh, thanks but that isn't necessary" replied Drew.

"Oh, I shouldn't have assumed, I am sure you have to get back to your family." Kate said feeling embarrassed again. She sure did that a lot around this guy. She was so out of her element and should just be quiet!!!

"I am not married actually, I lost my wife to cancer a few years ago so it's just me and my dad and my younger sister and I promised my Dad I would share the spoils of the day with him tonight, how about a rain check?" Drew said quietly with a slow smile but with a hint of naughty in those gorgeous blue eyes.

"I'm so sorry for your loss Drew, I lost my husband 10 years ago, so I understand." Kate said, trying to match his naughty look, but it probably just looked like she had a bug in her eye.

"Not a fun thing to have in common, is it? I'm assuming the oil is in your garage?" Drew said heading towards her garage.

"It is." Kate said following after him. But first she ran to the house to grab her phone, she ran back, and they exchanged information.

"Dinner sounds amazing actually," said Drew. "This past year Dad and I have been inundated with casseroles from a few of the lake ladies and I must admit I am a little tired of it, so a home cooked meal sounds amazing! But if I might, no casseroles please!!"

"Well, you are in luck because I love to cook! Just let me know when you can come, and I promise no casseroles!" laughed Kate.

After Drew left, Kate decided she had had an eventful enough day and decided on a light supper of a grilled chicken breast and some roasted veggies, she finished off the last glass of the wine that she and Jan had opened the night before. It was hard not to think of the handsome knight who had come to her rescue this afternoon and she laughed again at the 'breast incident.' But she didn't believe in fairy tales anymore. She knew they didn't all end well. Shake it off!! She told herself for the millionth time in ten years!

It was time to get to work. For the next several hours Kate worked on her children's book. She was halfway through writing book four so far in her series about a chipmunk family. Her publisher would be happy to get this latest book as the previous three had flown off the shelves. Grateful and humbled at her success, she couldn't wait to see where this next adventure took this little family of chipmunk's.

Working until she finished, she faxed off the latest book to her publisher and felt a huge satisfaction in getting it done. She always felt like she had just given birth after writing a book. Putting her heart into the pages could make one feel so vulnerable, but she had learned to not worry about what other people thought. The kids sure seemed to like her stories. She celebrated with a glass of her favorite Merlot. Now she would be able to do whatever she wanted until, hopefully the saga continued with these cute little creatures. Kate stood up and stretched and saw that it was after 1 am. Oh well, she thought, I can sleep in tomorrow, and she headed off to bed.

CHAPTER 3

Bang Bang Bang!!! Kate startled awake to the loud noise coming from downstairs, grabbing her robe as she raced down the stairs, she threw open the door to see Jan standing there. It was 9 am, and Jan was there for her morning coffee. Apparently, this was going to be a regular thing. Jan looked surprised and looked around Kate saying, "Oh, I'm sorry! Were you busy this morning?"

"Uh no, just busy sleeping, I had a late-night last night" Kate said cupping her mouth to cover her yawn.

"REALLY? What's his name? She said looking over Kate's shoulder as if looking for someone.

"Nope, just up later doing some work" Kate said smiling. "Come in, although I am still a bit sleepy".

Kate started the coffee pot and found some yogurt and fruit to go with their morning chat.

She went on to explain that she was a writer and was up late working on her latest project. Jan thought it was really neat that she did that and wanted to get some of the books for her summer grandkids she'd adopted from around the lake. During their morning coffee, Kate told her about the mishap with the boat the day before and about her handsome savior.

"I heard about him, he is so handsome! I know he moved here about a year ago on Goose Lake and lives with his Dad. I guess his wife died about 8 months ago." said Jan.

"Oh, I thought Drew said it had been three years." Kate said her brow wrinkling in confusion.

"No, I was talking about Drew's Dad, they are both widowers. But from what the ladies at the café told me, the father is a fit 74-year-old and plays golf 3 times a week and is quite the looker himself! I 've never met him though. Although I think I had seen him and his wife at Bingo at the church." Kate wondered if Jan had ever considered dating since her husband had passed. None of her business though. After talking of plans for the boat parade tonight, the ladies parted ways and got on with their days.

Later, Kate made a successful trip around the lake in the boat parade and even though she felt a little silly on the boat by herself, she managed to meet a few others who lived on the lake year-round. She was really going to like it here. Most of the people were her age and older and very nice.

Ashley, the owner of the bakery shop and her husband were part of the parade and she and Kate had a nice long visit after the spin around the lake. She surprised her by telling her she was only three cabins away. They all called them cabins, but these were all homes that could survive the harsh Minnesota winters. Kate really liked Ashley, she was a happy, bubbly extrovert and would really help bring Kate the introvert out of her shell a little. It was good to hang around happy people. It was infectious!

Feeling restless after putting the boat away, she saw that it was only 9 pm and having napped in the afternoon to make up for the lost sleep from being up so late, she decided to take a trip to town to see what it was like on a Friday night. Kate used to do things on her own, felt no qualms about going alone. When she got to the little town most of the shops were closed. Of course, the gas stations were open and as Kate drove through the town with her windows down, she could hear some music coming from somewhere, so she pulled over to locate where the noise was coming from. It sounded like it was coming from the bar called LU LU's.

"Well, I need to put on my big girls' panties and go in and have a glass of wine!" Kate thought to herself. Getting out of the car and looking both ways before she crossed the street, she found that there was no traffic and could have walked across the street blindfolded. Small towns!! As she opened the door the music and singing blasted her ears. There was a small stage at the back of the bar and on the stage was none other than Drew! He was singing! It was Friday night! Karaoke night!

Drew didn't see her coming in and she snuck to a little table in the back and ordered a Merlot. Drew was singing Michael Bublé's version of "Just the way you look tonight". Really? Was she in heaven?

Kate sat back while sipping her wine, closing her eyes, she got lost in the music and sentiment of the song. She sighed and opened her eyes watching Drew. He looked amazing in his jeans, black collared shirt, and cowboy boots. He looked like a handsome movie star. After the song ended, cheers and whistles erupted from the crowd and a red-faced Drew raced over to the bar......Kate watched what he ordered, a Merlot, and it was Coppola her favorite brand. As she looked around, she noticed that most of the people here were 30 to 60 years old and a nice looking 30 something year old woman got up and started to sing Chrystal Gayle's "Don't it make by brown eyes blue." She was really good! Kate could see Drew watching the lady sing and then turn and scan the room. His eyes lit up in surprise as he caught view of her. Slowly making his way through the crowd to her table, his face glowed when he got to her table.

"Kate, it's so wonderful to see you!!! I can't believe you're here!" He couldn't see behind him, but Kate could see the other women look her way in envy. She felt thrilled that he was at her table.

"Well, I sure never expected to see you here either Drew and wow! You sure can sing! Please join me?"

"I'd love to" he said as he moved the chair closer to her so that he could be facing the stage. His elbow rubbed up against hers and then the hot flash started her body would betray her yet again............ she was feeling things in her.... swimsuit area that she had not felt in many years.

This guy was turning her into wanton woman. As the song finished Lu Lu got up on the stage and announced that it was 10 pm and Karaoke was done for the night. As the bar emptied out it got quiet enough to have a conversation. Kate bent towards Drew and said, "so tell me about yourself Drew, are you the resident rescuer of damsels in this area?" This was her best try at flirting? That just sounded so dumb. Okay, she sucked at this flirting thing. Perhaps if she just shut her mouth. Drew leaned in and said, "Well, first I don't do THIS too often", he said with a laugh showing off his pretty white teeth. "This year I decided to make some big changes in my life. I retired from being a commercial pilot down in the cities and moved up here to be with my dad after my mom passed away. Tonight, was another thing on my bucket list, to move past the grief and try to start living again and to stop being a hermit, oh and I love to fish and to tinker." He said nervously. Maybe she wasn't the only one feeling nervous.

Kate looked up at the word tinker… "Tinker?"

"Yeah, I like to fix things, make stuff out of wood in my little shop and just general tinkering." He smiled warmly but his voice was a little shaky as he said it.

Kate said, "you seem a little too young to retire!"

"You know, after Christy died, I sat in the house alone between flights, my boys Joe and Sam are grown and have lives of their own. At 54, I was financially able to retire, and I wanted to live up here with my dad on Goose Lake.

He was lonely too after Mom died a year ago. He and mom bought a lot there twelve years ago and built their dream home together. It was too hard to stay in my other house. It held too many sad memories for me. Up here, all I had were happy memories, and I was ready to make some new ones." Gosh, it seemed like Drew really had his act together, Kate thought as she brought the wine glass up to her lips and sipped. "Wow," Kate exclaimed "you sound so healthy!! It took me years to figure that out!! I am so happy for you. I know how hard it was having stayed in the same house Ken and I had together. I wanted to provide some stability for the kids until they left home. But everywhere I looked I saw his essence. It's comforting at first, but then you realize that no matter how much you wish and long for them, they are never coming back. I guess that's part of the acceptance of death. You try to bring them along with you on a day-to-day basis, but life happens, and you start to let go a little at a time. That's another reason I moved up here. I needed to have a future without Ken and staying in the house we raised out family in was making that difficult." Kate continued. She told Drew how she felt ready to move on and hoped to maybe fall in love again. Wow with one glass of wine in her, she was blabbing to this guy like she had known him forever! She wondered if he thought she was hitting on him and she wasn't, but he gave her a long look and said, "Me too." Maybe he was hitting on her! He went on the say that he had not dated at all and had not been interested. He and his Dad, Neal got along great and spent hours playing chess, fishing, golfing, tinkering, going to music festivals and trying to help folks out when they could. Kate told him she thought is sounded like a great life. After paying their tab, Drew walked Kate to her car told her he would love to take her out if she was open to that. Kate reminded him about the dinner she had promised to make for him, and they agreed on Tuesday of the following week as Drew had told her he had plans for the rest of the weekend.

CHAPTER 4

After another great night's sleep and her morning coffee with Jan, Kate got to work looking for someone to come and help her do some things. She hired painters to give the interior of her house a fresh coat in every room, she hired someone to put in a new garage door opener and to put in a new back splash in her kitchen. They also painted the cupboards a fresh antique white. Everything looked fresh and clean. None of these people would fix her screen door and she had just laid it aside on the porch. She decided to try and tackle that job herself. She was going to need a drill and some paint for the door. Off to the hardware store again, she raced to town knowing the store closed at 8. She got there with ten minutes to spare. As she entered the store, the bell at the top of the door dinged and the squeaky floor announced her arrival.

"Well, hello pretty lady!" Grant made this greeting sound creepy, as he came out of his office.

"Uh yes hello, I need a power drill and some paint for my porch door. As he tootled off to gather those items, she picked out a paint color and brought it to the counter. Grant got there the same time she did and after she thanked him and paid for her purchases, she turned to leave. Grant caught her before she got to the door saying, "hey why don't you GRANT me a wish and have dinner with me?" He did the finger gun thing and wink and made a clicking noise with his mouth. Kate cleared her throat and quickly declined his offer as kindly as she could and scurried out to her car as fast as she could. What in the heck is with that guy? Did he really think that kind of thing worked on women? She could sure see why he was single. Who does that stuff? He was definitely not her type at all. Just as she was about to get in her car, loud music caught her attention out of the bar across the street. Much to her surprise, Drew spilled out of the bar with his arm around a gorgeous blond woman, looking much younger than herself and a body to kill for. They were laughing hysterically and took no notice of her at all. Furious at being so naïve as to think someone as handsome as him would spend a night alone, Kate got in her car and slinked down so as not to be noticed as Drew's car drove slowly by with said blond sitting next to him. Kate rested her head on the steering wheel and took a deep breath. 'It's not like we were even dating yet, we just met,' she told herself, but she kept thinking of the moment the other night at LU LU's when Drew looked in her eyes and told her he was looking for love too. I guess he was looking for it in a few different places. She felt that she had been duped and was so…. disappointed, Kate drove home with a small tear rolling down her cheek, determined to keep her head held high and get on with her life. She had better learn to have no expectations.

For the next few weeks Kate was busy with her new home, the painters were done, the kitchen tile work completed and the garage door now able to open without her getting out of the car. She felt satisfied with what had been accomplished. She gave herself a pat on the back for fixing the porch door, painting it and putting it back up all by herself. She had been to the antique store a few times to add some lovely touches to her new home and bought some twinkly lights to put out on her porch. She brought in some potted plants and flowers and added some new speakers so she could listen to music while out there in the evenings. Both of her kids had called to check in and promised to visit soon. All in all, Kate felt content with her life. Letting go of her hopes in Drew. She had made some new friends on the lake and continued to have coffee with Jan most mornings and went on the evening "put put's ". She did long for someone to share all of this with and she could see that as fall approached and then winter, things could get lonely. Maybe she needed a dog. Drew had texted and texted for days and wondered why she hadn't responded. After about a week he finally gave up. Kate wished him well with the blond but wasn't going to waste any more of her time on him. She really thought they might have had something special.

CHAPTER 5

As October approached, she took stock of her house supplies and decided it was time for a trip to the big box store to re-stock. A pleasant drive, the twenty miles passed quickly, and the leaves on the trees were stunning and she pulled into the parking lot of the Country and Farm Market. Grabbing a large cart, she gathered the items she needed. Her cart was stacking up high as she had paper towels, toilet paper, and other bulky items. Tipping her head off to the side so she could see around the paper tower, she headed towards the check out. As she waited in line, she heard someone come up behind her with a cart and she instinctively inched ahead. Out of the blue she heard a man called out to her.

"Kate? Is that you?" Kate quickly turned her head and looked behind her. Oh boy! It was Drew! Kate sighed dreading the conversation she didn't want to have.

"Yup! It's me!" she said somewhat sarcastically. Seeing him pull his small cart up next to hers, she cringed at what the next few minutes would entail.

"Kate, I've been texting you and got no response. I'm so sorry If I have done something to upset you! The last thing I knew we were to have dinner together several weeks ago. I wondered if you had maybe given me a fake number after I didn't hear back from you." Moving forward in line, Kate turned her attention to putting the contents of her cart on the belt.

"Look, Drew, I'm sure you're a nice man and I thought maybe we could be starting up a nice friendship, but I guess after I saw you come out of the bar with a gorgeous blond the night after we had made plans, I figured your social calendar was pretty full and you sure didn't need to be spending time with me. I just did you a favor and cleared up your apparently full calendar." She said turning back to the chore of getting everything out of her cart. After paying for her things, Kate said a quick 'goodbye' and headed towards the exit. Drew was right behind her having made quick work of paying for the few things he had in his cart.

"Kate, please! Let me explain" he said in a soft voice.

"Hey, you don't owe me any explanation at all! It's really no big deal" she said, putting her purchases in the trunk of her car.

"That gorgeous blond you saw me with is my sister Carolyn and she had come to town for day." He stood a few feet away, waiting for the truth to sink in....... oh.... my.... gosh, she thought, how dare I assume the worst about him when I don't even know him! She chastised herself.

Kate, slowly turned to look at Drew, his blue eyes burning holes in her flesh. Closing her eyes and slowly shaking her head, she whispered "I am so sorry I made a wrong assumption about you. Please forgive me. I'm new at this and I'm scared." Drew took a step closer until her was right next to her looking into her pretty brown eyes and said in a very sexy voice, "Can we just start over? No forgotten coats, no boat trouble with breast exam and no other ladies that are my sister?" he said with a little laugh.

"Drew, I have been single for 10 years and I really have no idea anymore how this all works anymore, I feel like a fool, but if you still want to get to know each other, I actually would like to start over." As she finished, she saw an older gentleman walking towards Drew, he looked like an older, shorter version of him.

"Hi, you must be Kate! I'm Drew's Dad, Neal. My son has been talking about you for the last few weeks, you should come by the place and let us cook some fish for you!" He beamed and gave his son a bit of a wink before walking to a blue truck a few rows away. Kate watched the older man walk away and yelled "Nice to meet you, Neal!" She thought well, he sure is a charmer! If he had been talking about her for the last few weeks to his Dad and he knew her name, she noted, she must have made some sort of impression on him.

"Well, that is my Dad!" laughed Drew. "He always says that life is too short to beat around the bush and if you want something you have to speak up about it! So how about it? Come back to the house with Dad and I and let us make you some pan-fried walleye. Dad and I can't eat all that we caught today anyway. Please? Dad is amazing at cooking fish!"

"You know what? I think I will take you up on your offer, nothing that I got today needs to be refrigerated so I will just follow you if that is ok, do you need me to stop and pick anything up for the meal?" She asked shocking herself that she once again was going to open up to him. Well, like his Dad said, life IS too short, and she knew that all too well.

"Thanks. Nah we have everything we need, except your pretty face, just follow us, I have the dark blue truck over there." He said, his eyes glowing with happiness. With twenty miles to think before getting to their cabin on Goose Lake, she went back and forth being nervous and excited at the same time. She really didn't know either of them! What if they were axe murders and she was falling right into their trap? Oh wait, Jan said she knew Neal and he was the retired police chief so that was unlikely. Was she really doing this? Her heart pounded with nervousness. She really wanted to like Drew, and she really wanted him to be a good guy. Her husband Ken was going to be a tough act to follow. Shaking off those thoughts she followed them the last mile down the pretty dirt road and at the end, it opened up to a beautiful very large cabin with upper and lower decks, an A frame shape that looked like it was right out of the magazine "Field and Stream." Surprisingly it looked like it had been landscaped by her son. Beautiful flowering bushes and large potted flowers and a pergola on the upper deck with grapes vines growing on it, the heavy fruit hanging low between the slots. WOW!! She noticed the large dock with a pontoon and a fishing boat, the yard beautifully maintained. She felt like she was in a dream and as she got of the car, Drew walked over to greet her.

"I am so glad you've come!!! Let's get inside and I'll show you around and then we can get some wine opened while Dad and I do our magic." he exclaimed.

"This place is absolutely gorgeous Drew!! I don't think I've ever seen anything quite like it!"

"Yeah Thanks! Dad worked so really hard all of his life in a stressful job, and this had been a dream of his for many years. He and Mom had planned this place to the letter, and they were so happy here, they loved having the grandkids here. They had been here 12 years and then one night Mom had an aneurysm and died instantly while in her sleep almost a year ago. This place is the heart of my mother, and you can see her beautiful touches everywhere." Drew had given her a lot of information in the last few minutes. He seemed a little nervous too and that made Kate happy that he was in the same boat as she was. Drew took her hand and led her down the slight slope to the house. Her whole body warmed to his touched and when he turned back and smiled at her looking like an older version of Taylor Kinney, she felt lightheaded. Is this what swooning feels like? She said to herself, a new experience for sure. After Drew gave her the grand tour, he brought her out to sit under the pergola and sip some icy cold Chardonnay. His Dad was busy in the kitchen prepping the fish. Sting placed on the surround sound speakers, and she could see Drew running around in the kitchen putting the fixings together for a salad. Seeing two good looking men in aprons and running around the kitchen cooking was an extremely attractive site. She had been instructed to enjoy the view, the music and that no she was not allowed to help. Pushing back into the thick cushioned couch, Kate let her head fall back and take in all the senses. She took in a deep breath and could smell some sweet honeysuckle, Sting crooned with his unique sandy but smooth voice and a gentle breeze tickled her noise. She had not thought her day was going to go this way, but she was not disappointed. When she opened her eyes, she saw Drew standing in front of her staring at her, his full mouth opened slightly, and his full lips looked so kissable she wanted to leap off the couch and jump on him! Whoa she thought, I wonder if he is feeling this same thing!! He sat down next to her, and he smelled amazing. He took her hand and held up his glass of wine and said, "cheers to a fresh start" and smiled gently. After they toasted, Kate convinced Neal, to let her at least set the table and it was decided that they would eat under the pergola and watch the loons on the lake singing their haunting tunes.

The conversation was light, and Kate found herself charmed by the older gentleman with kind eyes and a handsome face. He had a great sense of humor and had told a lot of funny stories during dinner. As a retired police chief, he was well known in the community and volunteered as much as possible.

Geez!! Kate thought, what a terrific guy! I wonder if Jan her neighbor… nope…. none of her business…still…but maybe….. After helping the guys with clean up and her many compliments to the chefs, Kate thought it best if she headed back to her place………. before she grabbed Drew and had her way with him in the woods! She was feeling a little heat from the wine she had with dinner. Best be on her way before she embarrassed herself again. However, Drew had a different plan in mind as he grabbed her hand and asked if she would watch the sun set with him on the couch on the upper deck. Kate could not say no to this handsome guy and sat beside him. A few minutes later Neal brought out two cups of coffee and then disappeared into the house.

CHAPTER 6

From the moment he had seen her in the coffee shop, Drew had felt an instant attraction to this chestnut-haired beauty. He had not even thought about dating since the death of his wife 3 years ago. He had met Nicole when he had needed to pick up a prescription at the local pharmacy where she worked at a technician. He had gone off to flight school and they married 3 years later. She continued working at the local pharmacy. They had had two sons and life was pretty good. Over the years Nicole started to have problems with his traveling as a pilot and being away sometimes for a week at a time and for a few years the marriage was rough. She had confessed that she had had a brief affair and they had gone to some counseling to save the marriage. The counseling had worked, and the last ten years of the marriage was better, but Drew had still had a hard time getting over the affair and he still loved her. He always wanted to be there for his boys and remained a great father and husband. When they found out she was sick with breast cancer, he had been her hero and champion as she went through chemo and then when her battle finally ended, he was there, strong for his sons. They had talked about everything, and both felt good with where things were when she passed away. She had begged him to find someone and to not grow old alone. At the time he could not imagine being with anyone else and felt broken and alone. He was content now on his own and he and the boys were tight. But now, with lives of their own and living down in the Twin Cities, he didn't see them as much as he wanted but he and his dad were happy building new lives and keeping busy. His Dad had always set such a great example of being a giver and someone who was always looking for someone one in need. Neal volunteered at the Senior Care home, playing games with the 'elderly' and often sneaking someone out on his boat for a day of fishing. He knew the secret of a happy life was being selfless and he showed it every day. Pulled back to reality, Kate's head had fallen on his shoulder having dozed off. Watching the gentle rise and fall of her chest, Drew felt a tightening in his chest. He had felt an affinity with her right away, and he wasn't sure why. An unexplainable connection with the gentle woman. Some kids at the house next door started lighting off some fireworks left over from the 4th of July and startled Kate out of her sleep. "Oh, my goodness was I sleeping?" she said yawning in a very sleepy soft voice.

"Hey, don't worry about it, I was enjoying every minute of it" Drew sighed.

"I guess that is my cue to head home." she laughed.

They stood up and he led her down the steps to her car. They quickly talked about what a great evening it had been. Drew asked if he could see her again and she was delighted and promised to answer his call or text next time. He told her he wanted to take her on a proper date, and both agreed to this coming Thursday evening. He asked if it was okay with her that he plan the date and she thought that sounded wonderful. She loved surprises. How romantic! There was a brief awkward moment right before she got in her car and they stood looking at each other in the twilight, he leaned in and gave her a light kiss on her cheek. She blushed and thanked him once again for a beautiful evening. As she drove away, she thought she could see his Dad peeking out the window. For some reason she thought that was just about the cutest thing she had ever seen. It was almost 10 by the time she got back to her place. She quickly called Angie and told her all about her evening. She and Angie talked at least once a day and her friend was thrilled to hear about her evening. With a promise to tell her everything about the upcoming date they ended the call and Kate fell back on her bed took and deep breath and sighed. She felt like a young woman again and let her mind wander at the possibilities with Drew. The guy turned her body to Jell-O. She felt things she had not felt in such a long time. The deep physical longing of need.........and she had some delicious thoughts about what he might be hiding under those clothes. Wait, WHAT??? She was 52 years old! She hadn't realized she could even feel this way again. And hey, she told herself she was still alive…and 52 isn't that old right? She chided herself….but just a little. She would stop beating herself up, it had been far too long since she had thought about herself. After finishing her nighttime bathroom routine Kate went to her top drawer and pulled out a new silky, beautiful nightgown, running her hands through the gorgeous fabric, she let it slide over her head. It touched her in sensitives areas as it slide down her body. She was always one to wear a cami and underwear to bed. But she felt like a part of her that had been asleep for years was coming awake again and this nightgown was the celebration of that awakening. Kate climbed into bed and drifted off to sleep with dreams of being in the arms of this sexy new man.

CHAPTER 7

Late October came in quietly and Kate sat out of her deck enjoying the crisp morning. Wrapped in a cozy big sweater and a comfy lap blanket, she sipped her coffee and had some time to thank God for her life, after spending some time in prayer, she got up to respond to her e-mails about her latest book. She was pleased to see that it was ready to go to print and that soon it would be on the shelves in books stores and for sale on Amazon. Grateful to not have to worry about finances, Kate contemplated on how best to use this extra money coming in. She was a simple woman and not in need of too much and had set money aside for her future grandkids. She really wanted to set up a charity in her husband's name and with this new money coming in for her books she considered some options to do so. She wondered if she could set up a foundation that helped kids somehow who were less fortunate. She really liked this idea and called her son Harry to discuss the possibilities. He had encouraged her in this direction and gave her a few ideas of how this might come about. Not one wanting credit for acts of kindness Kate made some calls and was able to get an anonymous foundation set up in Ken's name. Feeling like she had accomplished a lot that morning, she wanted to reward herself by going to the bakery and visiting with Ashley while she had a treat. With a nice cup of English breakfast tea and a chocolate croissant in front of her, she and Ashely chatted for a while and Kate shared her latest encounter with Drew. She had told Ashley about seeing him with the other woman and they giggled together as she told her that the 'other woman' had been Drew's sister Carolyn. Ashley knew Carolyn and explained what a terrific lady she was and that she hoped they would get to meet. On her way home Kate noticed a pop-up farmers market, called Doug's Digs, in the parking lot of the gas station and stopped in to grab some fresh tomatoes, fresh basil, zucchini, squash, some local honey, and a huge bouquet of zinnias. Zinnias were her absolute favorite fall flower and when she got home, she found several little vases and put them around her house. Excited for her first date with Drew tomorrow, she went through her closet wondering what she could wear. The evenings had cooled off some and she wanted to be ready for whatever the weather might bring. After 15 minutes of trying several outfits on she decided that after 10 years it was time to update her wardrobe. Knocking on Jan's door, she invited her to spend the day shopping with her and they headed to the 'big town' for day. Stopping for lunch, they shared stories of life's up and downs, and Kate told her she had a date with Drew. She was as nervous as a schoolgirl, but Jan reassured her that this was a beautiful thing! That it was okay to be excited about life again. That Ken would be so happy to see her this happy after having devoted the last ten years to raising fine children and so proud of her for writing the children's books. Kate invited Jan for dinner that night and made lemon shrimp linguini and an arugula and pear salad with roasted pine nuts and gorgonzola cheese in a light lemon vinaigrette. Kate had made some pumpkin bars with cream cheese frosting inspired by the smell of fall in the air. An autumn staple in Minnesota. It was hard to stop at just one. She was going to have to add some steps to her day to keep the pounds off from bakery habit and these fall treats. Wrapped in lap blankets, Kate had started the gas fire pit on her deck and the two women enjoyed a hot cup of coffee and companionable silence as the crickets chirped away the night's song.

After a restless night's sleep tossing and turning, thinking about her date, Kate finally got out of bed and went down to start coffee, her head felt like lead. The wondering all night long about how things might go tonight drove her almost to insanity. With a quick call to Jan, she told her dear neighbor that she was not up for the morning routine and said she was going to soak in the tub. Jan encouraged her that it was all going to be okay. Kate listened to some John Mayer as she soaked in the tub, and she let the music ease the stress away and it all seemed to flow down the drain after her bath.

After doing some laundry and some outside chores, she took a nap for an hour, read some of her latest novel, and then washed her hair and took some extra time putting her make up on. With a natural wave to her chestnut brown hair, she added some product to increase the curl and dried her hair using a diffuser. She rarely took this much time on her hair but tonight she wanted to look and feel her best. Taking her time on her makeup she added a light foundation, touched up her brows with a little color, added a bit of blush and some pretty taupe eye shadow that had flecks of sparkle in it, and then topped it off with several coats of mascara. She looked at herself critically and thought she looked pretty good for 54. She had kept out of the sun and took good care of her skin. Looking over some of her new clothes and decided on a pair of dark slim fit jeans, a lightweight burgundy sweater, and a short black boot. She dotted behind each ear with her favorite Channel #5 perfume and touched each wrist with the same. Adding a pair of earrings and a bracelet she felt ready to go. Kate decided to have a glass of wine out on the porch while waiting for Drew and put on some Frank Sinatra. She loved that era of music and the sound of big band. The wine helped a little to take the edge off her nerves. It felt great to be excited about a date again! She looked up at the sky and thanked Ken for helping her feel ready to move on.

Hearing a light knock on her door, Kate opened the door and took one look at Drew, and it took her breath away, her eyes almost popped out of her head. Drew smelled like "the sexiest man alive"! His blues eyes smoldered, and he looked good enough to eat in his black leather jacket, dark jeans, the crisp white dress shirt sticking out of the top of the jacket and some Italian leather shoes.

"WOW!!! You look stunning Kate!!" Kate told him he looked really nice too. (Was she drooling? She really needed to look into that!) He held out a bouquet of Zinnia's for her.

"Drew those are my favorite flowers??? I love them! Thank you!!"

He watched her walk into the kitchen and saw zinnia's all over her kitchen and living room and laughed out loud.

"Ha, ha, ha, Well I see that I guessed right but you do NOT need any more zinnia's right now!"

Kate blushed embarrassingly but said "you can never have too many zinnias!" She found a large mason jar and filled it with water, and she brought them out to the porch. She offered Drew a glass of wine and they sipped it slowly. He took in a deep breath and blew it out.

"Geez, I'm a little nervous!! I haven't done this in a long time!" He said.

She laughed and said, "oh I'm so glad you said that! I barely slept a wink last night!"

"Well, good then, we are both in the same boat! Let's just try to relax and have a good night." Parked in her driveway was a sleek black Mercedes coup. He opened the door for her, and she slid into the tan leather interior. It smelled like 'sexy man'. Once he got in, he put on some light music and took her hand saying, "I hope you don't mind if we go to a place that is about a half hour away? It's a little challenging to find good dinner food in a small town."

"Of course, not! Sounds wonderful!" Kate said nervously running her fingers through her hair.

On the way Drew was telling her he had been so nervous for the date and had not slept well the night before either and just about drove his dad nuts while getting ready for the date. Kate laughed and told him how great it felt to just be open and honest with each other about their nerves. Their easy way of talking took all the pressure off them and they talked all the way to the restaurant. Drew had chosen a really nice place on yet another pretty lake that was a supper club. With the large patio outside, three glass and gas fire pits were surrounded by intimate tables for two or four. Tiny electric lights and some dried flowers were strung over a metal and cloth pergola. It was a very romantic setting. The tables had white tablecloths on them and the small little lanterns with fake candles which created just right lighting for a romantic evening. Drew pulled her chair out just as a waiter came out and they chose a nice bottle of Merlot to start the evening. Both enjoyed a lovely meal and the conversation flowed like a gentle rain. Smooth and easy. Dessert came and went, and the staff swept the floor around them and continued to clear their throats in hint after hint of 'please go now'. Finally getting a chat from the waiter that they were now closed, Drew and Kate, laughed and apologized over and over that they had lost track of time. Drew gave him a very generous tip and glanced at his watch. It was midnight!!

"I'm so sorry I kept you out this late Kate!" Kate was also shocked to see how late it was and that five hours had passed since they had gotten there.

"Can you believe we have been here for 5 hours?" Kate said with surprise.

After starting the drive home, they both told each other how much they had enjoyed the evening. They had talked like long lost friends starting from their childhoods and growing to adulthood, through their marriages, kids, and death of their spouses. They had laughed until tears ran down their faces and even shed some tears as the ugly bits of life were talked about. By the time Drew walked Kate to the door she was ready for bed. After thanking him for the beautiful evening, Drew leaned in for a light kiss once again on the cheek. Her heart fluttered out of her chest and honestly, she told herself, she didn't know if she could handle more than that just yet. Kate went in the house and completed her nighttime bathroom routine and put on her new sexy night gown and spent the next hour going through the evening's conversation in her head. She smiled, she laughed and then out of the blue............ she started to cry. Big huge chest heaving sobs like she had not done since Ken had died. What in the world was wrong with her? She was happy! She was starting her new life!! Where were these tears coming from? Sometimes closing one door to open another could be painful. After several hours and an entire box of tissues, she finally fell into a fitful sleep.

Kate woke up early, with a dull headache which made her pause to even get out of bed. She looked at the clock on her nightstand. Ugh.... 6:45. She got up and dragged her feet to the bathroom, grabbed a couple of Tylenol, and headed back to try to sleep more, remembering her weeping fest. Kate startled awake several hours later to her phone ringing and she reached over to grab it from her nightstand. It was her friend Angie wondering how the date had gone.

"Hey there, I thought you were going to call me first thing and let me know how the date went with Drew?" Kate looked at her nightstand clock and saw that it was 11.

"Oh yeah, sorry I was going to call you this morning but woke up with a bad headache and ended up going back to bed for a while, in fact, your call woke me up."

"Wait," chortled Angie, "Are you hung over? That's not like you!"

Kate and Angie spent the next 2 hours on the phone while she talked in detail about how wonderful the date was. She also told Angie how she had lost it when she got home and probably gotten the headache from crying so hard. One of the thing Kate loved so much about Angie was how well she knew her. They had been friends for 30 years and she knew her friend inside and out.

"I know just what the deal is" said Angie with all the wisdom of Job. "You've put your life on hold ever since Ken died. You threw yourself and your grief into your kids' lives, working and paying the bills, never stopping for too long to just be………. I was so proud of you when you started to write about the chipmunks from your yard. I know how much joy these little guys brought to you. I loved when you could translate this joy to the pages of children's books to share that with them. I think this was another step away from the life that you and Ken had planned and then it didn't happen. You wouldn't date at all. You just closed off that part of yourself for ten years!! When you decided to make the move to the lake and fulfill your dreams, you were so busy doing and doing and doing and then you met Drew. Not looking for him, not needing him, at least in your own mind. All your friends have been in the background, hoping and praying and cheering you on in your new adventure. The wonderful time you had with Drew last night was the last nail in the coffin of grief, Kate. It's the end of a huge chapter in your life. You don't have to forget Ken and the wonderful life you two had, it's ok to start the next chapter in your life. That's why you cried so hard. My prediction is that, moving forward, you don't have to have Ken's death be part of you anymore. Just his life and the legacy that he has left behind in the children you both had. You get to be a beautiful, youngish (hey now!!!) woman again and get tingly feelings in your tummy and maybe some other areas too!! (Oh shush!!! YOU!!) and fall in love. Not all people get this chance so as your best friend I say go for it Sista!!!"

Little did she know, Drew had gone through a similar thing, although he had not cried all night. He had not really given much thought to dating and moving on and had grown content living the 'retired life' with his dad. He did have to admit that he was living the life of a 74-year-old instead of a 54-year-old. He was just scared. If he fell in love again, he might lose again. The Garth Brooks song, The Dance came to mind. "Yes, my life is better left to chance, I could have missed the pain, but I'd have had to miss the dance." He hummed the tune to himself. He wanted to dance with Kate, oh how he wanted to dance......After talking things over with his Dad, he felt better. His Dad, wise in his years, gently nudged his son to move forward. Drew called Kate later that morning and they shared what they had both been through. She loved the openness they had with each other. Kate felt a great deal of relief and Drew suggested they go dancing to start of their new 'let's be young and have fun' phase. He knew of a jazz band playing in the town 20 miles away and they agreed to go on Saturday night.

Happy that she had gone shopping, she called Angie and told her about her conversation with Drew and that they were going dancing Saturday night. Angie told her that she and her husband were going as well and that this band was really fun!! They were a band out of Wisconsin called 'The Johnny's.' Ashley told her she and her husband were going as well. Excited for her date, she cleaned her house, did some laundry, and even jotted down a few ideas for her   next   book. After a luxurious bubble bath and taking extra time to primp, she lathered her body with a new lotion and straightened her hair, Kate chose a casual but sexy black tea length dress to wear, she paired it with some sassy heels with a peep toe but changed into a more 'dancing' friendly lower pair of black suede short boots. Adding a pretty necklace and some earrings and a stylish black leather jacket she felt ready for her date. At the last minute she ran back up the stairs to her bathroom and dotted some Channel #5 behind both ears and touched each wrist with a slight drop. Now, she felt ready and excited for her evening. Just then she heard the front door inch open, and Drew's sexy voice call up, "Hello!!"

"Hi! I'll be right there!" With one last quick check in the mirror, she walked slowly down the stairs as Drew looked up at her…. his eyes were saying plenty, and Kate shared the same hunger she saw in his. After checking for drool, she grabbed his hand. Whew!! They had better get going or, well she didn't know what she would do!!!

They got to the bar and ordered some food and met up with Angie and her husband Tim, and Ashley and her husband Chris. They asked if they wanted to join them in their special booth reserved for band groupies. They accepted and slid into the booth. Drew ordered a Gin and Tonic and she got a white wine. It was a beautiful evening. The guys all knew each other just by living in the same town and seeing in each in man stores. They got on well and talked about common interests and planned to do some fishing together. Soon the band started, and Drew held her hand warmly under the table. His hand felt strong and warm, and she felt protected. A great fast song came on and he pulled her out on the dance floor. In fact, no one was seated. Everyone was out dancing, and the band interacted with the crowd making it even more fun. Three hours later, the three couples welcomed the fresh air and cooled off in the night air. After rehashing all the fun, they had had, they went their separate ways. While they walked the short distance to the car, Drew took her hand, and smiled at her with those smoking hot eyes. He opened the door for her, and she slid in and sighed as he went around to the other side of the car. Once he got in, they laughed and talked about what a fun evening it had been, and Kate confessed to sore feet since it had been years since she had danced. It was a nice ride home as they laughed at some of their goofy dance moves. He pulled in her driveway and Kate suggested he come in for some coffee. He gave her a long slow look and accepted. That man could burn a house down!!! Sheesh!!Once in the house, she got the coffee started. Drew went to look out the windows at the back of the cabin and sighed.

"Everything ok?" Kate murmured.

He turned and walked over to her in the kitchen. "Everything is more that I could have imagined Kate, you are a beautiful woman, you are kind, smart, you are once heck of a dancer, and I can talk to you like I've known you forever." Kate took a step closer, "I feel the same way, Drew." He leaned in for a kiss, on the mouth this time, she did not back away. His soft full lips moved slowly, and Kate moved in closer and put her arms around his waist. He backed away briefly and looked down into her eyes. Smoldering …….. HOT…...! He bent down again and started to deepen the kiss this time. They kissed like this for a while and the temperature started to heat up. Both were starting to breath very heavily. Drew pulled away gently and took a deep breath and blew it out like he was blowing out a candle.

"WOW!" he said. The evidence of his pleasure was clearly seen, and he cleared his throat and quickly turned to grab some coffee cups from the counter.

Kate laughed and said "Wow is right! I think maybe some ice water is in order instead of coffee!!"

He said, "yeah can you throw that on my pants!! I feel like I'm on fire!"

She loved that about him. He could make fun of himself and be honest about what was going on. They were both TURNED ON!!

"Should we talk? We haven't really had a conversation about this." Drew said as he leaned against the counter with a glass of ice water.

"Well, I know I am too old to get pregnant!" She giggled. "Let's take it slow Drew, we will know when the time is right. It's been a while for both of us and we aren't teenagers even though I sure feel like one right now!"

"Kate," he moved in front of her and took her face in his hands and tilted her head up and said

"I wouldn't have it any other way." They began kissing again and once again things really started to heat up. This time she pulled away…. and this time they both knew it was time to say good night before things got out of hand. It had been so long for both that she was tempted to go for it but, Drew was a special man and when they were going to be intimate, it needed to be special not just in the heat of the moment with no self-control. With one last good night kiss, he slowly let go of her hand and she watched him, and his fine bottom walk to his car............. He turned back and smiled and said, "were you checking out my butt?"

"BUSTED!! I most certainly was!" Kate said laughing. He laughed and drove slowly off into the night. Seeing that it was after one, Kate could not wait to call Angie until the morning.

That night, Kate had dreams.......and they were really good.........and she woke up with a smile on her face. She yawned and stretched and marveled over last evenings events. Well, mainly the last hour of the night. Drew was someone she could fall in love with. He was a solid guy. Genuine and they both felt like they had known each other forever. She had never had this kind of connection with Ken, although she had loved him, and they had a good marriage. But there was never this sizzling hot thing she was feeling for Drew. It was sexual attraction for sure and she was old enough to not be fooled into thinking that that alone was 'something'. Over and over, she recapped the conversations they had had. He kind of reminded her of someone she had known briefly a long, long time ago. Shaking her head, she leaped out of bed. Nope! Not gonna go there today!! Her phone buzzed and she saw that she had a text from Angie, her daughter, and Drew………. she saved the best for last. Angie wanted a call STAT, her daughter wanted to 'catch up' and Drew………. Drew said he could not get her out of his mind. Could steam come out of a phone? If it were possible, it would have been like a sauna!!She called her daughter and told her all about Drew and her date and Addie was really happy for her Mom. She wondered when she could meet Drew, but she thought it a little too soon since they had only had one formal date. With a promise to come and see her Mom next week end they ended the call warmly. Next on her list was to get back to Angie. This was more of a girlfriend phone call. There was giggling like schoolgirls and oh my gosh's and wow you really stopped? They talked about the intimacy part and about when to have sex with someone when you are older. Just go for it and hope for the best? That sure had not worked out for her in the past. But she was past menopause now and felt a freedom that comes with not being able to get pregnant. PLUS, it had been ten years!!! She was not sure she was going to be able to hold out very long but didn't want Drew to think poorly of her. Last night was a good indication of how hot they were for each other. He was also struggling to hold off. Her face turned red and hot as she thought about his, well his, 'tight pants problem.'

Kate had things to do and needed to stop this woolgathering. She went out and cleaned up the yard and cut the grass and the trees had started to change. Some leaves had started to fall, and she did a little bit of raking. She needed to blow off a little steam and it worked.

Starving, she went in for some breakfast and there was another text from Drew asking if he could come and pick her up for some fishing. She had not fished since she was a teenager with her Grandpa, and she had loved it. Drew told her he would be at her dock in an hour. He told her had had everything and to just dress warm.

Promptly, an hour later Drew rolled into the other side of her dock....... his eyes glued to hers with a big smile on his very handsome face. There was just something about him, like she had known him before, but that was impossible. He was so comfortable to be around. He hopped up on the dock and helped her into his fishing boat and after a warm greeting and a nice, yummy kiss on the mouth, they sailed away for the afternoon. What a wonderful day it had been relearning how to fish and with a patient teacher, she was able to catch a few sun fish and a walleye that was 19 inches long, a keeper! They stopped off at the Island and Drew had brought along lunch in a picnic basket that looked like it was from the 50's. In fact, he told her, it was his parents. He had packed the perfect romantic lunch of crunchy French bread, Havarti cheese, some crisp red grapes and some cotto salami. For dessert he had stopped at the French bakery and gotten two eclairs. He also surprised her with a lovely bottle of Merlot complete with plastic wine glasses. It was a weekday and with seasonal families back to school and work, the beach was deserted. Drew brought a blanket for them to sit on and they talked and laughed and shared more and more about each other. There was some more kissing and panting and stopping and laughing about that too. Soon, Kate had to go to the bathroom and was pointed to just the right tree on the Island to relieve herself. She was definitely not used to that but was a good sport about it. Otherwise, she would have wet her pants!! It was getting darker earlier now and they headed back to her place to clean and cook up the fish. She made a big salad, and they opened another bottle of wine. They enjoyed the meal out on her porch and snuggled under the lap blanket as the evening grew cooler. It was a great second date. Weeks turned into months, and Kate and Drew continued to date several times a week. They had had a big family dinner where her kids met his and she had met his boys. They were all around the same ages and got along well. Kate pulled out all the board games they had played growing up and watched as competitive natures came out. With food and drinks, a good time was had by all. Even Neal, Drew's Dad had come and had a great time. This all just seemed too perfect.

Christmas was coming soon, and everyone was busy prepping for it. Life on a lake in the winter is a whole different thing. People were active with ice fishing, taking kids behind 4 wheelers tubing, kids skating in between the ice houses that dotted the lake. It was a lovely place with all the activity. She and Drew would cozy up on the now enclosed porch, with a cup of hot cocoa to watch the winter wonderland. She had been working on her next book but had been so busy with her dating life that she really had to crack down and schedule time every day for it. There was no doubt in her mind that she was deeply in love. They had not said the words to each other yet but the way he looked at her…. I mean at this age you don't have time to play any silly games. She knew that very soon they were going to be intimate, and she couldn't wait.

CHAPTER 8

Her kids were due to come in the afternoon Christmas Eve and spend a few days with her for the Holidays. With her house decorated like a magazine including a beautiful blue spruce tree in the corner of the living room, the scene out of the French doors facing the lake it truly looked like a post card. It had started to lightly snow about 8:30 that morning and by midafternoon it had really picked up. Kate turned on the TV and saw that they were under a winter storm warning. As if on cue the phone rang and it was her daughter and son, saying they were not going to be able to make it. The snow down in the Twin Cities was already at 8 inches and it was falling at a rate of an inch an hour. They had started out and then turned around seeing car after car in the ditch. They were going to be staying at Addie's house and would come as soon as they got the roads cleared in the morning. Of course, she understood and would never want them to be in harm's way, but she looked around at what minutes ago to be a post card to just a sad empty house with no one but her. She looked outside again, and the wind had picked up, making it look like the snow was blowing sideways. She couldn't see across the lake anymore. The lights flickered off and on and she ran around to find candles and grabbed some blankets to make sure she would be able to stay warm if the power went out. Making a big cup of tea and eating a plate full of

Christmas cookies she put on a chick flick and watched the storm rage outside the window. Harry had texted that they had made it safely back to Addie's and made sure his mom was okay. Around 8 that night as the storm continued to rage, Kate felt a little frightened, the darkness out there didn't help. Kate drifted off to sleep finally and was awakened by loud banging on her front door. She woke up and saw that her house was dark and that the power had gone out. It felt cold in her house. She jumped up grabbing her blanket and throwing it around her shoulders ran to get the door. The door blew open and slammed into the wall behind and there stood a man with a rabbit hat down over his face and ears, a big Columbia jacket and some serious snow boots. "Kate? Are you alright? Our power went out as well and I couldn't text you, so I wanted to come over and make sure you are ok!" Drew, her knight in shining amour was here!!She grabbed him and pulled him into the house, and he shook off what snow he could. She hugged him tightly and told him that the kids couldn't make it because of the storm, and he had a similar story about his kids. She wondered why he was here if there was no power at his house and he explained that they had a generator. He then told her that he had one out in his truck and was going to go and hook it up for her. Through the fire department they had contacted people on the lake that stayed year-round, and she was the only one without a generator. Her dear friend and neighbor Jan had gone to Florida for the winter, so she was okay. After getting the generator all hooked up, Drew came back in to get warm. It was -12 degrees out and the storm raged on. True to his nature he had spent most of the afternoon helping people out of ditches and going house to house with his Dad to check to make sure their lake home friends were all ok. Kate could tell Drew was about to drop from exhaustion and once he got out of his winter gear, plopped on the couch in front of the fireplace. She brought him a hot brandy with honey and cinnamon, and he talked about his eventful afternoon. Kate made him a meal of the food she had planned for tonight's dinner for her kids, and he was thrilled to have roast beef, garlic mashed potatoes and some green beans and homemade rolls. He thought he had died and gone to heaven. Soon her house was toasty warm again and they sat on the couch companionably watching the storm. One thing led to another and soon they were kissing. With unspoken words, Kate grabbed his hand and lead him up the stairs to her bedroom. The rest of the night and into the wee hours of the morning they shared their love in the most intimate way. There was no need to rush, just the beautiful journey exploring one another. Drew had told her he was in love with her, and she was so in love with him.

This morning certainly was different than the others she had had here in her new lake home. She looked next to her, and Drew was on his side with his arm around her waist. "Good morning beautiful woman." He pulled her next to him and smelled her hair sending tingles down her spine. She leaned into him and sighed…….an hour later, they got up and took a shower together. He washed her hair and lathered her body with slow warm hands, as she did his. It was a magical time for them, and they relished every moment, each knowing how blessed they were to find each other. After cleaning up and sharing some more kisses they went down to the kitchen to see that the sun was shining brightly. Just then the phone on the counter rang and it was her son telling her they were on their way and should be there in about an hour. She had the phone on speaker, so Drew knew that he was going to leave soon. She gave him a huge cup of coffee and another deep kiss and wished him a Merry Christmas and made plans to see each other soon. He held her tightly and then leaning back he said "Kate Asher, I am totally in love with you." He left turning around to give her one last smoldering look. "Last night was beautiful." And before she got a chance to respond he left.

CHAPTER 9

Kate hugged herself in her big fluffy robe and relished in the thoughts of the events of the evening and the beautiful love making throughout the night. He was an amazing lover and played her body like a finely tuned Stradivarius. Each note played with precision and a passion the likes of which she had never known. Shaking herself out of her memories, she quickly saw that the power was on, and that Drew had shut off the generator. Grateful to have had it, she was also grateful to be able to have the loud thing shut off. They had gotten a foot of new snow and she noticed that as Drew left, he quickly shoveled the path to the driveway. The plows had already gone down her dirt road and the man who was pre-paid every year to do the driveways of the 'year rounders' was already done. She felt really spoiled but so happy and blessed. With the power back on, the furnace quickly heated up the house and she got the oven started for the day's meal. The kids were due soon, so she ran upstairs to put on some black leggings and a cozy sweater and dashed into the bathroom to fix her hair and makeup. "Mom?" came a voice echoing throughout the house. Kate ran down the stairs and hugged her son and daughter at the same time. "I'm so glad you had the smarts to turn back last night! That was a nasty storm. My power went out and Drew had to bring over a generator to keep the heat and lights going!" She exclaimed. Her son Harry felt bad. "Mom, I'm so sorry I didn't think of that for you when we were figuring out what you would need up here in the winter. Thanks to Drew you are warm and safe. I'll get one for you and bring it up here next weekend." Thanking her son, Kate she went on to explain that Drew was spending the day with his family. Harry grabbed some coffee and turned-on football as Kate put the traditional Christmas morning egg bake in the oven. She was finishing the icing on the almond puff pastry when her daughter came in to help her get the table set.

"Moooooom" she said in a sing-songy voice "Look at me Mom....... Mom!!! LOOK AT ME!" Her daughter whispered loudly.

"Uh, yes? what is it, Addie?"

"Mom you DID IT!!!!!!" Addie grabbed her mom by the arm and pulled her into the bathroom that was right off the kitchen. Kate didn't have much time to respond before Addie once said "Mom tell me everything!! You look radiant!! "

Kate said, "I don't know what you're talking about!" while blushing a deep red.

"I'm not a kid anymore Mom, start dishing!"

"I am not used to talking with my daughter about these things and it's really embarrassing that you even saw that!!"

"Mom I am a grown woman, and you were the one who taught me about the birds and the bees so get over it and tell me!! I am so happy for you! Drew is a great guy, and he is so hot!! It's been a LONG time Mother, and it's okay! "

"Okay, okay, okay, I'll tell you some, but no details! That is private and it's between him and me. Last night after you and your brother called to say you weren't coming…." Kate went on to explain how Drew had come over to bring the generator and then how things heated up and she invited him upstairs to her room. She went on to say that it was a magical night, and that Drew had said he was in love with her and she him. Her daughter was overjoyed at seeing her mother so happy. She had always put herself last and had been such a great single parent to them after their father had died. She and Kate had always had a good relationship and it only got better after Addie had been out on her own for a few years. Kate had friends who had daughters and knew those mother/daughter relationships could be a bit sticky. She was grateful and considered Addie a friend. They left the bathroom and went back out in the kitchen to finish the prep work for their Christmas breakfast and her daughter came up behind her and put her arms around Kate's waist. She whispered in in her "Oh Mama, you so deserve this second chance at love, and I am so happy for you, and I love you so much!" As Kate turned her eyes filled with tears, this was going to be the best Christmas she had had in a long, long time. The Holiday passed with ease and the New Year had come and gone. Harry had kept his word and brought up and new generator for her on Saturday but had tickets to go see the Vikings at the US Bank Stadium, so he didn't stay long. Kate and Drew spent the evening with a romantic dinner at her place, they danced, and murmured things quietly to each other. Both felt more blessed than ever and looked forward to more good times together.

CHAPTER 10

It was mid- March and Kate had gone for her bi- weekly visit to the French bakery and to visit with her friend Ashley. The two quickly caught up on the local news and each other's lives. The bell at the top of the door dinged and a man came in and went up to the counter to order a coffee. He glanced back at Kate, and she thought he look familiar somehow. He quickly paid for his coffee and left, and Kate thought no more about it. The following day she was doing some grocery shopping in the town and once again saw this man peering at her over the fresh produce. Once he saw that she saw him, he quickly went off in another direction. Once again, she had a feeling, she knew this man. By now she had become familiar with most of the people in town and didn't recognize him. Oh well, she thought, I don't know everyone and went on with her day. She mentioned him to Drew over dinner that night, he didn't think much of it but told her to keep her eyes open.

Kate had been wanting a new little table for her entryway into the house and decided to do some shopping at the antique stores in town. She found one in the second store and was delighted at such a find. While she was at the register paying for the table, she glanced out the window and there, sitting in a car across the street was that same man!! He was WATCHING her!!! She got a little freaked out. What does this guy want from me? She wondered.

Her car was parked close to the front of the store, and it was day light out, so she quickly put her things in the car and jumped in. From her front seat she looked around in both directions and the man was no longer in his car. Her heart pounded out of her chest with the loud rap rap rap in her driver's side window. It was THE GUY!!!! What the hell! She rolled her window down only slightly and said, "who are you and what do you want?"

"Um hello! Are you Kathryn Spencer?"

"Wow, you scared the bejesus out of me!! Who wants to know?"

"Well, my name is Jake Meyer and I think you are my biological mother" he said a shaky voice. Kate gasped, turned pale and promptly fainted. Her friend Ashely had seen the interaction from her bakery window and ran out to help. She looked at the man and said "Hey! What did you do to her? Get out of here or I'm going to call the police!!" The man backed away from the car and said, "I meant her no harm, I just had some news to share with her." He explained putting his hands up in the not guilty stance.

"Get the hell out of here before I call the cops", yelled Ashely. He reached in his coat pocket and took out a card handing it to her.

"I'm so sorry, here is my contact information. Can you please give it to Kathryn?" She took the card angrily but shooed him away. Once he crossed the street and got into his car and drove away, she was able to get Kate out of the car and helped get her inside and got her sitting down with a glass of cold water. Kate was the color of paper.

"What the hell was that all about Kate? Who is that guy???"

Kate, taking some deep breaths said, "I'm not sure! I have seen him around here the last few days, but I don't know what he wants".

"Well here," Ashely said handing her the card. "He gave me this to give to you." After she was feeling better Ashely went back to her other customers but was close by in case she needed anything. Kate's mind was going berserk right now. Time flashing before her, memories of another time, another life, another person, flashed before her. This could not be happening!! That part of her life had been put in a special box in her memory and then forgotten. A long-held secret. A place too painful to bring out. This was all too much for Kate to take in and she stood on shaky legs and told Ashely she was going to go home. On the way home she was trying to collect her thoughts. How did she know if this guy was her son or not? She had heard stories of birth parents being duped by con artists to get in with a family, especially one with money. How was she to find out if this guy was legit or not? Was there really a possibility that this was her son?? That was wonderful!! Or wait, what about her kids, she had never told another living soul. Oh, my lord, she thought rubbing her forehead. Kate was driving home in a trance; she finally noticed the red and blue lights in her rear-view mirror and slowly pulled off onto the shoulder of the road. She watched as the officer came up to her window. Lowering her window, Kate said, "Officer I'm sorry was I speeding?" He said "Kate!!! It's me, Carl! Are you okay? You were going 20 miles an hour in a 50!"

"Are you serious? I just got some shocking news Carl and I guess I wasn't paying attention to my speed. I'm okay now." She assured him she was okay and would pay attention to what was going on and he let her go after seeing that she seemed alright. This was the way it should be, her neighbor Carl, who just happened to be a police officer was looking out for her. Dragging her still in shock fanny into the house, she plopped on the couch and then the memories came.........Images of herself at the age 16 came into view like an old movie. It was a hot summer thirty-seven years ago. Kate had invited her friend Nicole to come to her grandparents' cabin on Lake Osakis for three weeks. It was a lot more fun when she was able to bring a friend along and her parents rarely went there. Some sort of falling out between her mom and her Grandmother, however, they let her go for three weeks every summer. The two girls had had a blast going swimming all day, and then Grandpa and Grandma would let the girls go to the club house every night for a burger and to play some pool. That summer they had met a group of kids also there for vacation and the two girls started hanging out with them every night. There was one guy in particular that caught Kate's eye. She went by Kathy back then.

"Hey Kath!" the handsome blue-eyed boy called from across the clubhouse.

"Oh, hey Andy! What's up?"

"A bunch of us are going to have a bonfire over at Kyle's and we want you and Nicole to come too! Stefani and Annie are coming too so the whole gang will be there!"

"I have to check with my Grandparents first okay"? Kathy used the pay phone to call them, and they gave her the 'okay.' They were pretty permissive and that is one of the reasons she loved coming here. She did however have a curfew and promised to be home by 11. As long as she stayed out of trouble, they gave her the freedom to do fun stuff while not under the watchful eyes of her very strict parents. After getting the ok, she and Nicole jumped in Andy's truck and off the went to Kyle's cabin which was on the other side of the lake. Other cars full of kids showed up right behind them and she was glad to see that Stefani and Annie were among them. Kyle's said his parents were gone for the night. Some of these kids were a little older than they were. Some 17- and 18-years old were hanging out too and the music was good, and the fire was hot, and the hormones were raging. Soon after the girls got there, cans of beer appeared from a cooler and the girls, like many kids this age, succumbed to peer pressure and drank some beer. Andy came and sat next to her and her friends. Nicole was dancing and chatting with his buddy Chad. Andy was so cute, and Kathy was really flattered that this guy was talking to her, and they really seemed to hit it off. They laughed and danced, and the beer kicked in and she felt floaty and delicious. There was a lot of flirting going on and around 10:30 the party started to thin out. Kathy was bummed that time had flown by. Nicole had told her that she was going to get a ride home with Chad, and they would meet at her Grandparents in about 15 minutes. Andy offered to drive Kathy home and she was thrilled! It felt good to be young, the windows down on a beautiful starry summer night and she loved the ride home in Andy's cool truck and he held her hand on the short ride back to her cabin when he pulled in the driveway, he asked if her could kiss her. She leaned into him as her answer. It was like going to heaven and back she thought, sighing. He asked her if they could hang out the next day and she was thrilled and said "yes!". Over the next few weeks, the two were inseparable and the same went for Nicole and Chad. It was the summer dreams were made of and they had a blast swimming, going to parties and doing some heavy petting. Andy was a great guy, and she was falling in love. After the three weeks were up, her heart was broken. She had to go back to her home in the cities and he was going to flight school. He was turning 18 in 3 weeks but promised to write and they talked about keeping in touch with letters and phone calls. The night before she was leaving, they had a special night planned. Grandpa said they could take the boat out to do some 'fishing' and they found a deserted beach at the other end of the lake. It was little more than a boat launch, but they found the privacy they were looking for. Kathy never thought about a plan. She was young and in love and living in the moment. The night turned into a night of passion, and things got out of control and Kathy lost her virginity. Neither thinking of the consequences. Andy had not planned this either and was also a virgin. He felt terrible and apologized over and over. He was scared that he had hurt her. She told him she was not hurt but felt scared too. Later that night they talked about how they wanted to keep in touch, but it was going to be a challenge. She had to finish her senior year of high school. With a last hug, he drove off with great regret. He should have been stronger, he really cared about this girl. He drove home with a heavy heart. The next day was miserable for Kathy. The two girls talked as they packed up to go home. Nicole was fine leaving Chad and they had just been friends that had shared a few chaste kisses. Kathy shared a little about Andy but had not gone into detail about the 'night'. There were no cell phones to keep in touch with back then, only phone numbers shared. Kathy was really sad on the way home and was glad to finally be alone when she dropped Nicole at her house. She wasn't looking forward to going back home where her parents had her under a microscope.

It was several weeks later Kathy (Kate) learned she was pregnant. She was terrified. In the first few days she and Andy had talked on the phone a few times and then he was gone to flight school. It was several weeks after this she found out that she was pregnant. She finally got up the nerve to tell her parents. School would be starting soon, and she didn't know what to do. She was petrified. She was a good student and not a party girl. After another sleepless night the big day came to tell her parents, and when she told them they were disgusted with her. Kathy's mom wasted no time getting on the phone with her mother and told them what had happened on 'their watch.' It was decided that Kathy would go and live with her Grandparents in Brainerd and home school while she waited for her unborn child. She would miss most of her senior year of school. What a mess she had made of her life in a split second. She was to tell her friends that she was going to live with her Grandparents because 'Grandpa had had a stroke and they needed her help.' This is the lie her parents told everyone they knew as well. Her parents had decided that she would give the baby up for adoption. They had already made all the arrangements and a 'nice family' would get her baby. Her opinion was never asked. She begged and pleaded with them and was ignored. She had turned 17 in September with no fanfare. "There is nothing to celebrate" her mother had told her. She knew best and told Kathy she would not let her ruin her life with a baby. The pregnancy was hard on her, she had puked for the first three month and although she and her Grandmother were close, she didn't feel she could share the loneliness she felt. It was four days after she was due in late April when she woke up to sharp pains in her back and a puddle on the floor of her room. Her grandparents took her to the hospital. She gave birth to her beautiful son alone. He was quickly taken from her and put into the arms of his adoptive parents waiting impatiently outside her room. She had not even been able to hold him, she wept for days. Her grandparents brought her back home a few days later after her milk dried up. She had never heard from Andy again. The phone number which she had tried over and over again had been disconnected. Kate went back for the few short weeks of her senior year and was able finish high school with her other classmates as if nothing had happened. Her mother had told her not to say a word to anyone as it would ruin their reputation in church. Whenever she tried to bring it up with her mother, she would just say "NO!" She had no one to talk to and had to put the memories away…. for good. Several months later she left for college and had met Ken her Sophomore year, and they had gotten married at 20 years of age. A year later her son Harry was born, and Kate continued to go to school while her son went to day care. She had graduated with honors in English. She had never told anyone about this baby. She had never told anyone about Andy. It was a secret she would take to her grave or so she thought and had put all of the pain of this in a box in her mind. Of course, she would think of this little boy through the years and on his birthday in April, she would cry quietly to herself when she had a moment. She had always wondered who got her boy. After Ken died, she decided it was time to lay the guilt and shame aside and forgive herself for getting pregnant. It had taken a lot of work and through God's love for her she was able to do that. She had never stopped praying for her baby boy, she had never stopped thinking of him.

Hours later, she became aware of where she was, still sitting on her couch with her coat on, it was dark now and her face was wet and her eyes swollen with hours of crying, there was snot everywhere. Her doorbell rang, she looked a fright she sat up quickly and ran to peer through the window to see who it was, please, not now she thought, I have nothing in me right now. But there stood Drew......she let him and in he brought her in for a huge bear hug.

"Honey! What's wrong? I have been texting you for hours!!!" She sobbed into his Columbia jacket, and he led her over to the couch. He went to the kitchen and made her a cup of tea, for as we all know, tea makes everything better. She took this time to go and wash her face. After she drank the tea, Drew put his arm around her shoulder and said, "whatever it is, I'm here and we will get through this together." Kate took in a deep breath and slowly blew it out.

"I have a secret to tell that I have never told anyone." Then she talked and talked and talked spilling out what she had never told anyone.......... about the baby she gave up so many years ago when she was just a girl. Drew was a good listener and took it all in while continuing to hold her.

"First of all, Kate, thank you for trusting me enough to tell this painful story. It must have been devastating! I'm so sorry that you went through that alone and that all these years you haven't been able to tell anyone! That is so sad! Your parents.... I'm speechless about that." He held her closely trying to absorb some of her pain. "So today this guy shows up out of nowhere and says he is your son?

How do you know? Did he have some sort of proof? I wonder how we can find out who this guy is before you contact him.? Maybe my dad can help? Maybe we can have the guy do a DNA test?" Kate leaned into Drew, feeling his strength and acceptance. She felt embarrassed at the thought of having his dad know about a part of her life that was so incredibly painful. Oh, Lord, she thought, what am I going to tell my kids? This was a good news, bad news situation, and she had no clue how to move forward or what the heck she was going to do. She felt like this could ruin some lives or maybe enhance it. She laid her head in Drew's lap completely emotionally spent.

"Honey, you need to get some sleep, we don't need to figure all of this out tonight. I suggest a hot bubble bath. We can talk all this over in the morning and if you want, I can help you with any decisions you make or do whatever you need me to do. I just ask that you don't meet with this guy until we know who he is for sure." Kate agreed with this plan. He ran upstairs and found her bubble bath and got the tub started for her. After an hour soak, she came out and found Drew sitting on her bed. He had a tray with a bowl of chicken noodle soup and some saltines. "Kate, you need to eat a little something and then, if you want me to leave I will, but I'm not sure you want to be alone tonight." Kate walked over to the bed and Drew took her in his arms. "I'd love for you to stay Drew." She climbed into bed ate a little bit of soup. Drew set the tray aside and then joined her in the age-old spooning position and she fell instantly asleep in his cocoon of safety.

Kate woke up with the dawn that morning, she needed a hot shower and snuck out of bed, so she didn't wake Drew. She let the hot water sooth her weary soul. She rejoiced at the idea that she might have met her son, but now what to do with that? Maybe the DNA idea was the way to go. What about her other kids? How would she tell them? What would they think of her? She has raised her kids in her Assemblies of God church. Raised them to be moral and had given them 'wait for marriage' lectures. She just had wanted to spare them the sorrow she had been through. Feeling like a hypocrite, she let the water run cold, she had prayed about the situation. God would provide the strength for her; she knew but she was still scared. She dressed in some flannel sweats and a big fluffy sweatshirt, slid her feet into some warm, thick socks and made her way down to the kitchen for a cup of strong coffee. Kate could hear Drew stirring upstairs and realizing how hungry she was she made some eggs and toast and bacon for them and nibbled on some blueberries, while waiting for her guy to come down. She really didn't know if she could have gotten through last night without him.

CHAPTER 11

Jake sat in the hotel room with his head in his hands, wondering if he had made a mistake coming here. He was 36 years old and alone. He knew his news had come as a big shock. He also knew that she needed some time to process everything that this meant. He also knew he had some half siblings too and wondered how or if she would tell them about him. Would she want him in her life? Was it too much to hope for? Would they be angry for messing up their lives? He did not have a bad life at all, it had just felt like something was missing. He had been in a few serious long-term relationships but his lack of ability to commit always brought them to an end. At some point he did want a family but not until he had found his mother and got 'the' question answered. 'Why did she give me up?' He thought meeting his mother and finding out why she had given him up might help him be able to just bloody get on with it. He had gone through all the fears that adopted kids have. Wanting to see who his 'real' family was. His adopted parents had been great. He was the oldest of three. The other two were their biological kids and looked just like his parents. He was tall, and his dad was short. His parents were blonds and had brown eyes, and he had dark hair and blue eyes. He had gotten so tired over the years of the comments about how he was the 'mail man's kid.' Over the last few years, he had talked to them about how to find his biological mother and while they felt a little sad, they fully supported his efforts and his Dad had helped him find a private detective. Jake was an air traffic controller and made plenty of money with his job, but the money was pointless without someone to share it with. He had dated plenty and was a good-looking man. He lived alone now and had a dog named Whiskey. He had taken himself out of the dating world for now. He needed to see this journey to the end, whatever that was going to be. He grabbed a book he had brought and lay back on the bed to try to occupy his mind while waiting for his 'mother' to contact him. He wondered if she would. He thought he would give her a few days and then if she didn't contact him, he would go home and try to get on with his life. He had taken a week of vacation and hoped that was enough time to sort this out.

When Drew got home that night he was conflicted in his emotions. He was glad Kate was finally able to tell someone her secret. She had never told anyone. What a terrible secret to carry with you all alone! He wanted to help but certainly understood her not wanting to bring his dad into it. This was a very private matter and what if this guy turned out to be a fraud? He thought it best to be supportive but not tell her what to do. He felt very protective of her and didn't want her to get hurt. This was a big deal that could have big consequences for her family. He loved her so much and wanted her to know he was there no matter what.

Jake had not slept well even though the bed was good, and the room was nice. He had worried all night long that he had made a mistake. He meant no harm to his birth mother, and he feared she would not contact him. He had texted his dad and told him he had met 'her.' His dad encouraged him to hang on and to wait a few days and let the news sink in. He grabbed a hot shower, dressed, and decided to go to the bakery. The bell rang as he entered into the heavenly smells of the place, and he ordered his favorite almond Danish with slivered almonds and a tall hot black coffee and sat by the window in the front of the bakery. He stared out the window wondering what the day would bring. Ashley, seeing that this was the young man from the other day, thought he looked sad. She walked over to him and laid her hand on his shoulder startling him out of his deep thought. "He buddy, my name is Ashley and I noticed you from the other day with Kate. You're the guy that said something at her car and freaked her out. I gotta tell you, if you mean her any harm, she has this whole town backing her up. What is your intention with her?" Jake dropped his head and shook it back and forth with his eyes closed and then looked up at her.

"Ashley, my name is Jake and I mean Kathryn no harm at all. It really is a private matter. I would appreciate some privacy please." He said quietly. He didn't look like a murderer, but then they never do….

"By the way, your Danish is delicious." He said with a weak smile. She backed away slowly returning to behind the counter as other customers came in. She gave him the two fingers to her eyes and then pointed them at Jake in the 'I'm watching you' gesture.

"Thanks!," Ashley said loud enough for her customers to raise their eyebrows at her.

CHAPTER 12

Kate heard the familiar sound of Drew's truck as it pulled in the snowy driveway. He jumped out of the truck and as he approached her door, she swung it wide open for him. Unexpectedly, he grabbed her in a bear hug and lifted her off her feet. She felt completely loved. She giggled like a schoolgirl. What does that even mean? Kate suggested they make some coffee, have some lunch, and talk things over. She told him she was just about to text Jake and see if he wanted to come over and talk. He was honest with her and told her not to jump right into this. He brought up bringing his dad into this once again telling her that as the former chief of police he could pull in a favor and do a background check on this guy first. It wouldn't take long to see if he was a criminal or not. Then if he was clean, they could suggest meeting this guy in town, in public the first time and suggest doing a DNA test. Kate thought this over. She was seeing this from a different angle. Her son!! She would so love to get to know him, and her emotions were running high. She decided to take Drew's advice. She had met Drew's dad several times. He was not the kind of person to go spreading rumors around town. She gave Drew the go ahead and they called his Dad and with the speaker on. Drew explained the situation to his dad. True to his nature, he assured them discretion and haste, there was no judgement in his voice. While they waited to hear back from his Dad, Kate filled bowls of her homemade chicken soup and warmed up some ciabatta rolls. She brought a tray out to the living room with the food on it. Drew had put on the gas fireplace creating a cozy atmosphere. They ate in companionable silence. The soup had been something she had always made when her kids got colds. It was comfort from head to toe and the perfect thing to eat today. It was early April and while the warm sun melted the snow every day, it rarely got above 50 degrees. They both stared out the French doors facing the lake, watching the icicles melt. It was strangely relaxing.

It was nearly two hours later and in the late afternoon when the call came in from Drew's dad.

"The kid is squeaky clean, had a speeding ticket at 18 and has no criminal record. He has been working at the Minneapolis International Airport for the last ten years as an air traffic controller. His parents are decent folk who have lived in Brainerd for the last 60 years. They have two other kids ages 30 and 28. A boy and a girl, the boy is younger. I can't say if this is your son or not, but he is not a criminal. I think those guys make a good living too so not the type to be running a scam in my opinion. I would definitely get the DNA testing done though just to be certain. You will both need to get the test."

"Hey Dad, thanks so much for doing that. We'll talk soon, love you!" Drew said.

Kate took in a deep cleansing breath and blew it out slowly. "Well, we are one step closer. This is all so scary! I guess the next step for me is to meet with Jake and see if he was any proof. I have thought about it, and I want to meet with him on my own. I'll ask if he will meet me at the bakery. There are always plenty of people around, so I don't feel afraid to meet him there. I hope you understand."

"I do understand honey, but would you mind if I was outside in my truck parked down the road? "

"Actually, I think that is a great idea. I was going to ask you to drive me anyway."

HELLO JAKE, WOULD YOU BE ABLE TO MEET ME AT THE BAKERY IN CEDAR PINE TOMORROW MORNING AT 9?" She texted the phone number from the card that he gave her with his contact info on. It was just an index card cut in half with his name and number handwritten on it. Several minutes later she got a bling on her phone that she had a text message from Jake:

I WOULD LOVE TO MEET YOU AT 9 AT THE BAKERY, THANK YOU!

Her life as she knew it was about to change.... forever. She trembled in fear, or was it excitement?

That evening, Drew picked up some rotisserie chicken from the deli in the grocery store and some mashed potatoes, he also grabbed a bag of frozen greens beans and a can of Pillsbury biscuits. He could grill anything, but cooking was not a skill he had mastered. He wanted to pamper Kate a little and she was delighted to see him bring all of this in and set it on the counter. He got her a glass of wine, settled her at the counter facing the kitchen and put on some Credence Clear Water Revival while he set about getting things ready for dinner. He got the oven heated up for the rolls, and she directed him to a cookie sheet, and he started plating up the still warm chicken, mashed potatoes and put the steamtable greens beans in the microwave. The timer went off on the oven and he pulled the fresh baked biscuits out of the oven. Kate giggled to herself. The was the first time anyone had ever 'made' her dinner and she was delighted with his thoughtfulness. He sure looked adorable as he brought her a plate filled with the delicious food and she waited until he could join her. He grabbed her hand and told her that everything was going to be alright. She was so happy to have him here and felt his strength and encouragement. They finished their meal, and he cleared the dishes and made light work of washing the few dishes, putting them in the dish drainer to dry. While Kate watched, she was having a few naughty thoughts, and smiled. She felt so safe with him and although she was nervous about tomorrow, she felt grateful to have such a great guy in her life. They shared some tender intimate time that night and as Drew kissed her at the front door, he told her how much he loved her and confirmed the plan to pick her up at 8:30 the next morning. He needed to go back to his place and get some things done and talk with his dad. Kate tossed and turned that night and finally got up and read for a while. It was going to be a long night. She finally fell asleep after 3 and woke up nervous, afraid and excited. This was the day she might finally meet her son.

Kate and Drew pulled up in front of the bakery at 8:45. She wanted to get there a little early and be there before him. Hugging Drew, she got out of the truck. The sun felt so warm today and she turned her face toward warmth, the heat felt like a kiss from God. This helped take some of the nerves away. She had spent some time in prayer today and was at peace.... for the most part.

Entering the little bakery, Kate made her way to the counter. Ashley was there to greet her and asked if she was okay and explained her encounter with the stranger from the other day. Kate didn't want to tell her what was going on yet, so she told her friend that he was meeting with her that morning and she would fill her in later and to trust her and please keep it to herself. If that was even possible in a town this size, since everybody knew everybody. Oh well, she just could not figure all of that out right now. Kate decided on a few eclairs and a large cup of Earl Grey tea. She took her plate and tea to a table near a corner of the bakery. There were only four tables and the other three were filled so that took care of that decision. Taking a bite of the delicate pastry filled with sweet cream, she savored the feeling in her mouth. Closing her eyes, she let the feeling permeate all the way to her toes. She heard the bell on the shop door ding and in walked Jake. He scanned the shop and met her eyes and walked over to her. Standing up Kate suggested he go and grab something to eat and drink. He declined a pastry but ordered and large coffee and headed back to her table and sat down. He was carrying a large leather folder. He was shaking.

"Thank you so much for meeting me, I'm so sorry for how I told you the other day, I really didn't mean to scare you! I had just been so excited that I finally found you that I didn't even think." Jake said rubbing his forehead. Kate smiled gently at him. "It was quite a shock Jake. Let's just start over, okay?" Reaching her hand out towards Jakes she shook his hand. Trembling from both fear and excitement Kate started the conversation. "I think it's important for me to see some proof for both of our sakes. I am going to be really up front with you. I had a background check done on you to make sure you are legit and not someone out to scam me. I know that might sound a bit rude and harsh, but I felt it was necessary since you're a stranger to me. I would also think that for both of our sake we should get a DNA test done. That will take any doubt and question out of this. I am hoping and praying that you are my son." Kate eyes were filled with tears. Jake took in all that this lovely woman was saying. He admired her for getting the background check on him. He would have done the same thing in her position. He sipped some of the strong hot coffee and opened his leather folder and pulled out a piece of paper he pushed it towards her.

"Actually," Jake said, "I don't have a problem at all that you did a background check on me. You are right, I am a stranger. Let me share some of what I have found that leads me to believe that I am your son. I hired a private detective after I reached a dead end. From my adoptive parents I was able to learn that I was born in St. Joseph's hospital in Brainerd Minnesota, that is where I was raised. My birthday is April 26th, 1986, and the name of my mother on the birth certificate was Kathryn Elizabeth Spencer age 16. The place for the name of the father was left as 'unknown'. Kate's face grew hot as she listened to Jake, she WAS Kathryn Elizabeth Spencer, her married name was Asher, she had just turned 17 on September 3rd. She had never seen the birth certificate. She would have put a father's name down. It must have been her parents who had provided the information. She had been so young and so naïve. She was surprised they had even used her real name. Jake went on to say "the birthplace of the mother is St. Paul, Minnesota and her birthday is September 3rd, 1969. Through the private detective I was able to come up with the names of her parents and their addresses and the schools she went to." He took another piece of paper out of the leather folder and slid that over to her as well.

While reading, Kate mouth dropped open as she read about her life. The house she grew up in and the schools she went to, there was even a re print of her senior picture on another piece of paper from the folder. She looked up at Jake and said with tears in her eyes. "Jake, that is me," her eyes filled with tears. "I'm your mom!" She took out her phone and texted Drew quickly and told him she was safe; the guy was legit and had solid proof that she was his mom. Kate took a deep breath and began to tell the story of long ago..........and the beautiful summer where she met Jakes dad............she didn't leave much out but kept the intimate details to herself. She went on to add her deep sadness at having been forced to give up her baby boy, the fact that she never got to hold him and that she had prayed for this baby boy every day of her life. She talked about Jakes father and how much they had loved each other even though they were so young, and their time together brief. She told him that when she found out she was pregnant, she had lost touch with Andy and her parents had made sure he never called again. She went through her history of her marriage and that Jake had a sister and a brother. She talked of her husband's death and what lead her to move up here. Jake then told her about his life with his adoptive parents and that they had been good to him and treated him like their natural son. He told her he had felt a void in his life and why it led him to seek her out. He wondered if she would be interested in locating Andy. That was next on his list of things to do. But seeing "unknown" on the birth certificate left him at a dead end.

"Jake, I'm embarrassed to say that I don't really know too much about him. I know he was from the twin cities. But we were so young and didn't really talk about our lives and backgrounds. His name is Andy Johnson. Such a common name so I'm not even sure how you would go about it. I have never tried to find him. I don't have any other information for you about him."

"Well, if it's ok with you I'd like to bring my private detective in on this. Do you know if he lived in St. Paul or Minneapolis?"

"I'm pretty sure he went to Central High school, and he is two years older than me."

"That's something!" Said Jake.

She told Jake that she needed to talk to her kids and would like some time to do that before they planned for him to meet them. He was happy that she was even considering this. After promising each other to keep in touch, Jake asked if he could give her a hug and she of course said it was fine. She was holding her baby boy for the first time, who was now about 6'2. It was the strangest thing to be holding him. It was an instant connection and instant unconditional love. When they pulled away, there were tears in both of their eyes. As Kate left, the sky look like a cement truck had spilled all over the sky and the clouds hung heavy. She felt the heaviness in her spirit as well, thinking of what she was going to tell her kids. She got into Drew's truck and sighed heavily. "Drew you are so patience waiting all this time for me to come out, thanks" she said grabbing his outstretched hand. She went over what Jake had told her and he still thought it might be a good idea to get the DNA tests just to be 100% sure.

"While I am so happy to meet my son, I am terrified to tell my kids."

"Kate," he said gently, "I understand honey, everything will work out the way it's supposed to. You have great kids. They might welcome a new brother. You have to trust the process. Let's get you home sweetie."

That night Kate got on her knees and prayed. Talking to God as if he were right there with her, she poured her heart out and felt better afterwards. It was all in His hands. She texted both of her kids that she needed to talk to them about something important and that she wanted it to be as soon as they could both get away. She reassured them that she wasn't sick or anything, just that she had some news she wanted to share. Both kids got back to her with questions, but she said she would answer all of them when they came. It looked like this coming Saturday would work for both of them and she suggested they come to her house for lunch. Saturday was only a few days away and she was a bundle of nerves and cooking relaxed her so she baked cookies, made some Bolognese sauce and decided she would make pasta for the lunch. Italian food was her favorite and the kids loved it too. It kept her busy and she cleaned her house from top to bottom even though with just her there it wasn't dirty. Drew had taken her out for dinner last night and he was able to get a laugh out her with some lame dad jokes. He reassured her again that everything would be okay.

Kate woke up with the dawn on Saturday and she took a long hot shower and prayed again. She went through her closet and tried to figure out what to wear and after throwing half of her closet on the bed she finally settled on her well-worn comfy jeans and a light blue sweater. The days were warming up and 60 degrees was in the forecast for the day. She looked at herself in the mirror. She wanted so much to look like herself as a mom. She bent her head over and shook out her damp hair and added some mousse to it and then added some light make up. She grabbed a pair of white tennis shoes and headed to the kitchen. Her friend Jan had gotten back and few weeks ago and they had had coffee a few mornings. Kate had not told her what was going on. She wanted to wait and see how all of this turned out before she shared such a personal story. She made a cup of English Breakfast tea this morning and broke off a piece of fresh brioche and added a little butter and strawberry jam and took it out to the porch to stare at the Lake. The ice was finally gone, and the water once again danced in the sunlight bringing hope to her soul. She had done most of the food prep last night, except for cooking the spaghetti noodles. She had made a mixed green salad and had a loaf of fresh French bread sitting on the counter ready to go in the oven. She had made the chocolate cake that both kids loved. In her mind, if she made all these yummy foods maybe the kids would take the news better. Drew called her and they talked for about half an hour and she him she would call after the kids left. At 11:45 the kids got there, and she brought them into a big hug. They had been the three musketeers since Ken had died. That set her to worrying again as the three were now four. Both kids, who were now adults clamored her with questions. "Kids, let's just get something to drink and let me get the food on the table, I will explain everything after we eat." After getting the kitchen cleaned up the kids were impatient to hear what she had to say. She led them over to the living room and had them sit on the couch while she chose the big comfy chair across from them....

"I have a story to tell you both and I want you to let me get to the end before you have any questions, okay? "

"Mom, you are scaring me," said Addie

"Well let me get started then" ....when I was a young girl......

CHAPTER 13

As she emptied her heart to her children, she wasn't sure what kind of reaction to expect. Her daughter crossed the room and sat at her mom's feet and held her hand as the part of the story got to where she got pregnant. Her son's eyes looked sad like a basset hound. She couldn't let that deter her from telling the rest of the story. She had to get it all out and let the chips fall where they may. When the end came, Jake revealing who he was, she took a big breath and blew it out......

Her daughter was the first to respond, "Oh Mama!!" She reached up and hugged her mother tightly. "Now I understand why you have not been close with Grandma and Grandpa. How awful that you couldn't even hold your baby!! I can't even imagine what you went through and that you had to go through it without being able to tell anyone! All these years!" Her daughter wept on her mother's shoulders and Kate couldn't help but let a few tears of her own fall. Her son just sat there staring at her. "Harry?" Kate saw that he was looking at her but couldn't get a read on what he was thinking. He stood up and walked to the kitchen, opening cupboards looking for a cup. Kate got up and walked over to him and got a cup out for him. "What do you want in this?" He said, "I don't know, do you have any booze?" Kate paused and rubbed his back....... "Harry, talk to me, please." He broke away from her and opened the fridge, grabbing a beer and walked out onto the deck, he stared at the lake and took long swigs of the beer. Addie went over to her mom and put her arms around her. "Mom, give him some time to process, it's a lot so just let him be for now. I have some of that to do myself. We love you so much! "Kate decided to give the kids some time alone, so she walked down to the dock and decided to take the pontoon out for the first time this spring. It was a chilly 60 but it was sunny, and she grabbed a jacket on her way out. Taking a slow ride all around the lake, Kate let the sun soak into her soul. She had dropped the big bomb on her kids and now she needed to trust that she had done the right thing. She questioned herself repeatedly about whether she should have told them sooner, but there was nothing she could do about it now. As the saying goes, 'it is what it is'. She saw a few neighbors out in their yards doing some spring clean-up and getting docks and boats ready for the season. She waved and smiled as her boat slowly took her around the lake. It was about an hour later when she gently pulled the boat back in and saw both kids sitting on the deck above. Kate walked up the slight slope to them and by the time she got to the deck both kids stood up and hugged her.

"Mom," Harry said," I needed a minute after you told me I have a brother, in fact that is all I heard at the time. I had to go over your whole story in my head. Can we sit?" Kate turned on the gas fireplace and then they all sat around in a circle. Her daughter brought out a bottle of wine and some glasses and handed the poured wine to her mother and brother.

Harry talked more. "I guess at first I felt really betrayed by you that you had kept this from us all these years. Did you not think that this day would come where your kid would come looking for you? All these years you must have wondered what would happen if he did. On the other hand, I am now the middle child" Harry laughed a little trying to lighten the mood.

"You are right Harry, I should have told you both sooner, I guess I was afraid of rejection, and I was also scared that after your father died that if you rejected me that I would be alone. It was selfish of me. I'm sorry for the way things have come about. I was also ashamed that I have never stood up to my parents and gotten information about the adoptive parents and fought harder to find my son. I had never told anyone, even my best friend. In fact, I guess you could call me a coward." Kate dropped her head in shame and tears rolled down her cheeks. Her kids had always seen her as a strong woman, she had been such a champion after her husband had died. She had dug in her heels and became a survivor rather than a victim. She had been scared out of her mind to be alone. So, she got busy to keep from really feeling much of anything. Addie came over to her Mom and being the sweet loving girl, she was said

"Mom, it's all going to be okay, we just have figure this stuff out together. You are NOT alone. We are all in this together. Her son got up and pulled his mom up gently and into a group hug.

"We love you Mom and it's just gonna take some time for us all to adjust to this news and to the fact that we have a brother! I might really like having him around!" The wine certainly was helping to keep the mood light and helped them get through this moment. Kate remembered a bible verse that said, "when a man is full of sorrow, give him strong drink." This was definitely a moment like that. They kept talking through the afternoon and it was like old times in the kitchen with them making a fabulous dinner together, listening to great music, and laughing about old times. Both kids wanted to set up a time to meet with their new brother and Kate texted Jake to see when he would be free again. He had gone back home and back to work. He had texted back that he was free the next weekend and plans were made for them to all meet at her house and weather permitting have a barbeque. Both Harry and Addie decided to stay over, and they took a sunset cruise around the lake together. Harry took over as captain of the boat and they cranked the tunes as they putted around the lake. Kate texted Drew that things had gone well and that the kids had decided to stay over, and she would fill him in after the kids left in the morning.

Kate woke up early and went downstairs and got the coffee pot going and decided to make the kids their favorite breakfast of French toast and bacon. The smells of the bacon brought both kids out of the bedrooms and she loved seeing their sleepy heads. Memories flooded her mind of many other mornings like this, and she wondered if somehow Jake could have been part of this from the beginning. She now wished she had shared her secret with

Ken, wondering if he could have helped her find the boy and been able to be part of his life somehow. You can't live with regret though because you can't go back and do the thing you wished you would have done. It was a waste of time. She had to move forward and try to make the best of things the way they were now. The kids ate and she talked to them about what she was just thinking. She wanted them to learn from the mistakes she had made. They were such great kids and she had asked them to forgive her and when they left that morning, she felt so proud of her kids and hoped that she could give herself the grace they had given her. She texted Drew and asked if he could stop by later. They spent the rest of the day together and she told him everything that had happened the night before. As usual, he was a patient listener and supported her in every way he could. Kate kept in contact with all three kids during the week and brought her laptop computer down to the screened in porch to work on her latest chipmunk book. She was feeling good about this next chapter not only in her life but the lives of the little chipmunks in her book series. Big puffy white clouds filled the sky and robins sang and all the birds were returning from their winter homes down south. She loved watching the finches, the orioles and the hummingbirds come back, and it reminded her that she needed a trip to town to get food for all the bird feeders she had around the yard. After getting back from town she filled the feeders with black sunflower seeds and suet and made a huge batch of simple sugar for the hummingbirds. By dinner time the hummingbirds ate hungrily at the feeders. It was balm for her soul to watch these pretty little birds. Drew came by on Wednesday and they had a romantic evening, with some fishing on his boat, and they had packed up a picnic to eat while fishing. She had brought a bottle of Shiraz and they sipped wine from plastic wine glasses. The fishing was great that night and they had a string full of sonnies and perch. They spent the night together and made love on the porch with the night sky lit up with millions of stars free from the ambient light of the city. She was madly in love with this man! He was such a sweet man and just the perfect combination of strength and sensitivity. Life could make a person better or bitter and she knew that Drew had had some tough times in his life but instead of it making him bitter he let life teach him and make him the kind man that lie next to her. She cherished him with all her heart. He had agreed to come on Saturday and that was okay with the kids too…. all three of them.

Kate had gone to town to visit with her friend Ashely and brought her up to speed on what had been going on her in life. Ashley freaked out when she told her the story but hugged her friend and was overjoyed that the 'guy' was really her son and not some creep that was out to get her. The next day she met with her best friend of 30 years and told Angie the whole story top to bottom. At first her friend was really hurt that she hadn't told her about the son she had given up for adoption so many years ago. Angie had had some drama in her own life when she found out that her husband had a daughter that he didn't know was his and was being raised by his older brother.

Turns out, that during a brief break up when they were young adults, he had a brief relationship with his brothers now wife and that had resulted in a child. The girl at the time had been going through a rough time and had slept with a few different guys and wasn't sure who the father of this girl was. His brother married her when the little girl was two years old and had adopted her and they went on to have two children of their own. He had raised the little girl as his own but as she got to the late teen years, she wanted to know for sure who the father was, and this created a huge crisis in the family when Angie's husband was asked to provide a 'sample' for DNA. Angie had not known that her husband and her now sister-in-law had spent a teenaged drunken night together. Angie and Tim found out that he was in fact the girl's biological father. It had been a challenging time for them and their marriage and for their other three kids. They now had a sister/cousin. After a year of family counseling, they had made it through this crazy episode. So, naturally she felt betrayed by Kate. Kate told her how her kids felt the same way. She apologized over and over to her dear friend and understood that it was on her that she had not trusted anyone enough to tell her 'secret'. Both she and Angie had learned over the many years of friendship, that love, and forgiveness and acceptance was key to maintaining that friendship. They had had a few bumps in the road and like a long marriage their relationship had been through similar seasons. They would get through this too. Angie wanted to be there for Kate as Kate had been there for Angie when she had gone through her crisis. Both women hugged and

Kate promised to keep her in the loop of the saga going on in her life. Sometimes they felt like their lives were like a bloody soap opera. It was her turn to live out her drama scene and Angie would be right there with her to get through this next part.

It was late April and Kate couldn't have prayed for better weather for the barbeque today. It was going to be in the mid-seventies which was rare for this time of year. Drew came over early to get the ribs started on the grill. He was a master at grilling and his ribs were to die for. He made his own rub and then glazed them with Dr. Pepper every hour to give them a unique sweetness. Kate was busy in the kitchen making potato salad, coleslaw, and her famous baked beans with crispy crumbled bacon, some white vinegar and tangy mustard and a few dabs of ketchup. Both her kids loved this old family recipe and she hoped Jake liked them as well. She made a carrot cake and frosted it with cream cheese frosting. She then got to work on her charcuterie board. She pulled out some salami and had learned how to make meat roses on Pinterest, she laid out a variety of soft cheese and crackers and opened a jar of Mediterranean olives and pour them into a small bowl. She cut up a few veggies and pulled out the cool wooden board Drew had made for her when he had cut a tree down in his yard. Sanding it down for a smooth finish. She began arranging the items on the board in a decorative way, and added some pistachios, almonds, a small jar of honey, some crackers and some small, sliced bread she had picked up in the deli section at the grocery store. She topped it all off with some crisp red grapes and backed away to look at her masterpiece. Being creative in the kitchen was always so relaxing for her. In the meantime, Drew had filled a cooler with ice and put several kinds of beverages in there including beer, some of the new vodka drinks that came in cans and some water as well. She had both red and white wine at the ready in case anyone wanted that instead. He had just come in from basting the ribs another time and looked around the kitchen. It looked like a massive bomb had gone off. Kate looked up at him and saw his expression and looked around the kitchen seeing for the first time the mess that came along with her creativity! This wasn't the first time she wished she had someone to go behind cleaning up the aftermath that her creative storm caused.

"Uh, yeah so this is how I deal with stress. I make giant messes in the kitchen when I am cooking. I'm all done making the messes now!!" She laughed as she saw the horrified look on his face.

Drew took a deep breath and said "holy moly Kate!!!! You have enough food for twenty people!!! He laughed at her and said "looks like the demolition team has left and your kids will be here in two hours! Let's do this!!!" She went over and hugged this hunk of a man and kissed him passionately. Drew pulled her back and said "you cannot be kissing me like that when we have this giant task in front of us!!! You make me crazy woman!" So, they got to work, and it only took 30 minutes for them to get the mess cleaned up. Most of the dishes fit in the dishwasher. Kate ran upstairs to take a quick shower while Drew finished up in the kitchen. She decided on a navy-blue sun dress with white flowers on it and decided not to fuss with her hair and threw it up in a messy bun. She added some light make up and touched up her lips with a light gloss and dug through her closet until she found some strappy white sandals. It was breaking the 'don't wear white before Memorial Day rule,' but she didn't care. She was getting nervous as she looked at the clock on her nightstand. The kids would start arriving in less than an hour. She got downstairs and saw Drew out on the deck sitting on one of her comfy chairs and came up behind him and put her arms around him and kissed his cheek. She inhaled deeply the scent of her man and she felt a stirring…but there was no time for that…. he turned around and pulled her into his lap. She felt like a teenager as he kissed her and told her how much he loved her. She told him the same and they both sighed at the same time and then laughed that they had sighed at the same time. He asked how she was feeling about the kids meeting today and she told him she just had to let it happen and see how things went. No one would go hungry that was for sure!

Jake got there first and had brought his mom a big bouquet of flowers. He was nervous as well and Drew shook his hand and introduced himself. He had seen Jake from afar when he had parked outside the bakery that day but had never actually met him. Jake took the beer Drew offered him and they sat and chatted for a bit. Kate ran around looking for a vase for the beautiful flowers. Drew kept looking at Jake and couldn't shake the feeling that he seemed so familiar to him. They talked about work a bit and Drew told him he had been a pilot based out of the Twin cities for the last 30 years. He told him he had probably landed his plane on many occasions, and they laughed they had probably talked many times over the years via radio as his air traffic controller. Kate saw her kids coming in the front door and ran over to hug them. They hugged her back but also brushed her out of the way a bit to hurriedly go out to finally meet their long-lost brother. Kate followed after them and Jake immediately stood up and greeted his brother and sister. It was a little awkward at first, but they soon settled into telling stories about their childhoods and compared notes about how they were similar in some of their traits. Kate saw some of both of her kids in Jake now that they were standing next to each other. Kate went into the kitchen to bring out the snacks and set them on the table and drinks were served to everyone as they sat down to talk. Drew just kept staring at Jake as he reminded him of someone....... someone from long ago.

The day went off better than Kate could have imagined. The meal was a big hit and the kids made plans to hang out down in the cities together. It was close to 9 when everyone finally went home, and Kate fell into bed completely exhausted. She thought Drew might stay over but he had been strangely quiet for the last few hours of the night. He kissed and hugged her, and she thanked him over and over at how helpful he had been. She didn't think she could have gotten through the day without him. She fell into a dreamless sleep. Drew however was freaking out a little. He drove home faster than her should have and ran up the steps to the house. His dad was in the living room watching his favorite Clint Eastwood movie and asked Drew how things went, and Drew briefly told him that things had gone well. He quickly said goodnight to his dad and took off for his bedroom. He ran to his closet and on the top shelf he moved several boxes aside until he came to the old blue shoebox hidden in the back. He pulled it down and several other boxes fell on him in his haste. Kicking those aside he took the blue box and went and sat on his bed. Slowly taking the lid off, his past slammed into him. He hadn't looked at this for many years. He dumped the box on the bed. There, he saw photos from his high school, old ticket stubs from bands he had seen and a few ribbons from when he ran track. He spread them out all over the bed until he found what he was looking for. It was a faded, crinkled, photo, dull with the passing of time. He went over and turned on the light next to his bed and held the picture up to it. He brought the picture up close.......... he was looking at a 35-year-old picture of Kathy. He couldn't believe what he was seeing, it was the spitting image of Jake...or how Jake would have looked at that age. Jake had a beard now so it was easy to see how he would have missed it. Was this a weird coincidence? What the hell!!!!! There was no way he could wait until morning. He jumped up and grabbed his coat and put the picture in his pocket and ran downstairs past his Dad.

"Hey is there a fire? What's going on?" Neal shouted after his son.

"I'll explain later Dad! I promise!" Drew yelled as he sailed out of the house. Drew drove like a bat out of hell back to Kates's house and banged on the door. The house looked dark, but it was only 10 :30. Bang bang bang! He beat on the door. He was not thinking right now, only feeling. His heart was pounding out of his chest. He saw a on light come on in the house and he tried to be patient as he waited for her to come to the door. Kate peered through the peep hole and slowly opened the door. "What on earth is going on Drew? Is something wrong? Is your Dad, ok?" She said breathlessly. Drew, knowing he looked like a crazy man said "Kate I have something I need to talk to you about and it's really important, I couldn't wait until l tomorrow. Can I please come in?"

"Of course, Drew!" She pulled him and made some coffee. Drew paced back and forth waiting for her to come back with the coffee. She gave him his cup and they both sat down on the couch next to each other. "Drew, talk to me! What's going on???" Drew took off his coat and took the picture out of his pocket.

"Kate, today when I saw Jake, there was something about him that seemed so familiar to me. At first, I chalked it up to the fact they we had probably passed each other a time or two at the airport. But as the afternoon went on, he reminded me of *someone*. It was of a girl that I had known the summer after I graduated from high school. I had spent a few weeks at Lake Osakis with a buddy of mine. I met a girl named Kathy. We were nuts for each other! I tried to stay in touch, but her parents told me to stop calling the house because she had gone to live with her grandparents." He then pulled the picture out and handed it to Kate. He watched the blood run out of her face…….

"Wait" Kate said, she began to tremble as she looked down at the photo. It was her. "where did you get this picture of me? I was 16 here and this is in front of my Grandparents cabin?"

Drew took her in his arms. "Kate, THIS is the girl I fell in love with and lost touch with! I used to go by Andy!" Kate pushed Drew back. As the truth finally began to sink in, her eyes grew large, and tears poured down her face. "Drew!!! Are you saying that out of all the people in the world, I move up here all these years later and we meet and fall in love and the universe has seen fit to bring us together again?? This is too fantastic to even believe!" They jumped up at the same time and like little kids held each other jumped around in circles. Pulling back and staring at each other. They looked so different than they had a kid. They had been drawn to each other right from the start and now it all started to make sense. It suddenly dawned on Kate, and she screamed. "Oh my gosh Drew, that means…………that means you are Jakes father!"

Now it was Drew's turn to freak out. He had been so excited to find out that Kate was 'his Kathy.' He hadn't even known that he had fathered a child…. the suddenness of all the news caused Drew to sit down. He was taking deep breaths. Oh My God!!! Jake was THEIR SON!! Kate and Drew, or Kathy and Andy spent the rest of the night together talking, laughing, crying, and going over her story again, she had not gone into any details before when she had told him she had given a baby up for adoption. Now she told him everything about when she told her parents and how she had to go live with her Grandparents and been alone when she gave birth to her son. They wept together at what might have been. How her parents had filled out the birth certificate and listed that father as 'unknown'. How her son had been passed to his new parents and how she had suffered all these years not telling anyone. He felt terrible for her. He would have married her. Had he known. All of the would haves and should haves have passed through his mind. What a night this had been after an already dramatic day. They finally fell asleep in each other's arms as the sun came up. It was near one pm before she felt Drew stir next to her and he brought her in close to him and they spooned. "I love you so much Drew, I never really stopped. I just gave up my 'little girl' dream of ever seeing you again."

"Aw Katie, my love! It's a miracle that we have found each other again and now we have our son!"

Drew left after a cup of coffee and needed to go home and fill his dad in on what had transpired. He had texted his dad last night and told him he was staying at Kates', and he would explain everything when he got home. Jake's birthday was just a few days away and they wanted to tell him the news together. So, they invited him to join them for supper at the River's Edge Supper Club. They had decided together to tell him first before they said anything to their kids. Drew had the daunting tasks of telling his other boys that they too had an older brother. Jake drove to Kate's house that Saturday as it was planned so they could all ride together. It felt strange to Jake riding in the back seat of the car. He felt like a kid again. Drew had made reservations and had chosen a private table in the back of the restaurant that looked out over the Apple River.

A man, dining alone like he did every Saturday night, watched from across the room. A ruckus was taking place right in front of him. A woman and two men seated almost in front of him were in some deep conversation. The looks on their faces were both euphoric and the young man seated with them looked shocked. He wondered what that was all about.......

TO BE CONTINUED in Book 2

Made in the USA
Columbia, SC
25 September 2021